Dog Friday

Dog Friday

Hilary McKay

Margaret K. McElderry Books

Margaret K. McElderry Books
An imprint of Simon & Schuster Children's Publishing Division
1230 Avenue of the Americas
New York, New York 10020

Copyright © 1994 by Hilary McKay
First published in Great Britain 1994 by Victor Gollancz Ltd.

First United States edition 1995

The text of this book is set in Garamond

Printed in the United States of America

10 9 8 7 6 5 4 3 2 1

Library of Congress Cataloging-in-Publication Data

McKay, Hilary.
Dog Friday / Hilary McKay.—1st U.S. ed.
p.   cm.
Summary: Ten-year-old Robin Brogan is determined to keep the dog
he finds abandoned on the beach from being impounded by the police.
ISBN 0-689-80383-4
[1. Dogs—Fiction. 2. Police—Fiction. 3. England—Fiction.]
I. Title.
PZ7.M4786574Do 1995
[Fic]—dc20   95-4446
CIP
AC

Dog Friday

one
● ● ● ● ●

"Robin!"

Deep in his dreams, Robin recognized his mother's voice and began to drag himself awake.

"He's been fast asleep!" said the nurse. "Bless his heart! How old is he?"

"Ten and a half," replied Robin's mother, and almost added that he was much too old to be blessed but then thought better of it. "Hello, Robin," she said, and her voice was so anxious and gentle that Robin woke completely and sat up in sudden alarm. For one awful moment he thought that his mother was going to turn mushy on him.

"Robin, you are a howling idiot!" said his mother, and Robin sank back on his pillows with a sigh of relief.

"Hello, Mum," he said. "Sorry if you were worried!"

"If!" repeated Mrs. Brogan. "If! Look at you!"

"He looks fine now we've tidied him up," protested the nurse, shocked by Mrs. Brogan's unmotherly remarks.

"Well, thank God I didn't see him before, then!" said Mrs. Brogan devoutly, and for a moment the nurse wondered if she dared ask her to leave. Luckily for everyone she was called away before she could make up her mind.

"They won't let me get out of bed," said Robin rather forlornly.

"You poor old thing," said his mother, gingerly kissing the top of his head. "And now I've gone and shocked the nurse!"

"She's nice really," said Robin. "She brought me a bottle of orange juice that she pinched off a dead patient!"

"Robin!"

"Well, that's what *he* told me!" said Robin, nodding toward the next bed. "Mum?"

"Yes?"

"What do I look like?"

For an answer Mrs. Brogan fished in her handbag and handed him a small mirror.

Robin gazed into it at a face he hardly recognized. Two black eyes and a bandaged head. One side of his face dead white and the other covered by an enormous gauze pad. His left arm was bandaged and strapped across his chest, and what was that around his neck? Surely it couldn't be true! He wriggled his legs experimentally and found that it was.

"A NIGHTIE!" exploded Robin. "A WHITE NIGHTIE!"

"Serves you right," said his mother, "and anyway, it's not a nightie. It's a hospital gown."

"It's got pink stuff round the neck," said Robin. "Get it off me!"

"It's very fetching," his mother told him, "and no

more than you deserve. Stop worrying about your looks and tell me how you are feeling."

"Terribly hungry," said Robin, after having searched through his symptoms for the least alarming. He would no more have frightened his mother by describing the terrible mixture of pain and numbness that was assailing him than she would have explained what the sight of a policeman waiting by a police car at the garden gate had done to her. For Mrs. Brogan it had been like a replay of a two-year-old nightmare; it had even been the same policeman. This time, however, he had been waving and nodding and smiling as she approached, so that even from a distance she would know that it was not fatal. He must have remembered too.

"Terribly hungry," repeated Robin.

"I'm not sure I'm allowed to feed you," said Mrs. Brogan.

"Why not?"

Mrs. Brogan pointed to a huge notice hung over the door which read,

DO NOT FEED THE ANIMALS

in multicolored letters.

"That's just a joke," said the small boy in the next bed, and he watched admiringly while Mrs. Brogan unpacked cookies and chocolates and potato chips and bananas. He had been in the hospital for so long himself that his family had stopped arriving with unlimited supplies of food. They brought apples and educational puzzle books instead.

"And," said Mrs. Brogan with a flourish, "I brought

pajamas! Two pairs! And your bathrobe and slippers and some day clothes and your library books."

"How long will I be staying?" asked Robin, appalled.

"Goodness knows," said Mrs. Brogan. "Hours, probably! Now let's get you out of that nightie!"

"There!" she said a few minutes later, when Robin was respectably dressed and had borrowed her mirror to inspect his wounds again. "All done up like a dog's dinner! Oh, sorry, Robin! Sorry, Robin! Sorry, Robin!"

This time the nurse, who had returned at just the right moment to catch this remark, really did ask her out.

"It's quite okay," said Robin as she hugged him good-bye. "It was funny!"

"Good old lad!" said Mrs. Brogan. "I'll be back tomorrow. Sweet dreams and no worrying! You'll feel much better in the morning!"

It was one thing to order sweet dreams, but it was quite another to receive them. Long after the rest of the ward was fast asleep the events of the morning played themselves through over and over again in Robin's mind.

Someone on the beach threw a toy for a dog to fetch. The dog did not see where it landed and searched frantically along the sand until Robin Brogan found the rubber ring and picked it up.

A moment later the dog saw the toy and ran toward it, and Robin, startled by the speed and size of the animal, jumped away. Instead of dropping the ring his fingers clutched it even more tightly. Then the race began.

The dog could run faster than Robin. He could not outdistance it. At the beginning of the chase he had been surprised and alarmed, but as it went on his fear increased and he started to panic. When the dog drew closer and he could hear its breath tearing in and out of its body, terror came over him in a blackening wave and he did not hear the voices calling or see the rock that tripped him up. The only thing he was aware of in the whole world was the dog. When Robin fell it sprang.

The hospital kept Robin under observation for three whole days in case anything happened to his head, but nothing did.

"It's the Easter holidays!" Robin reminded the doctor. "They are all going to waste! It doesn't even ache!"

"We don't take chances with heads," the doctor told him. "Not even solid rock ones like yours must be." Very gently he guided Robin's unbandaged arm up to feel the bump on his forehead and it was so spectacularly enormous that Robin stopped protesting.

"How's the arm feeling?" asked the doctor.

"Still numb from the injection," Robin replied.

"Enjoy it while it lasts!" said the doctor ominously and moved on to Robin's neighbor, who had both legs in casts up to his hips. The two of them seemed to be very good friends.

"I see you haven't managed to escape yet," Robin heard the doctor say.

"Neither have you," pointed out the boy.

"True, but at least I get paid to be here." The doctor caught Robin's eye and winked at him over his patient's head. Robin winked back and cheered up a bit.

"Will I get out for my birthday?" the boy was asking.

"All you people want is to get out!" said the doctor. "It would hurt my feelings if I had any! When's your birthday?"

"June the tenth," replied Robin's neighbor. "I'm getting a skateboard."

"I don't know why I bother!" exclaimed the doctor. "I should have been a butcher! Much more job satisfaction!"

"Shall I get out then?" persisted the boy, "or don't you know?"

"I'll tell you what I do know," said the doctor. "If you get a skateboard on June the tenth you'll by lying right where you are now on June the eleventh!" And he marched out of the door.

The boy looked after him, grinning.

"I'm not really getting a skateboard," he confided to Robin. "I just said it to tease him. I think it's good here really!"

Robin grinned back at him and thought privately that it was lucky his neighbor was enjoying the hospital because it was obvious that he would be staying for a long time yet.

The three days that Robin spent in the hospital seemed the longest in his life and he was glad to get home again even though home, after the shining hospital ward, looked more dilapidated than ever. It was half of an old Victorian house on the Yorkshire coast. Originally it had been one large family home, built by Robin's great-grandfather and called Porridge Hall. Robin's great-grandfather had made his fortune selling rolled oats and he had been so proud of his excellent porridge that he had called his home after it. The name was cut into a large white stone built into the front of the house. Robin's mother often looked ruefully at that stone and thought it a pity that the porridge money was the first and last ever to come into the family.

Some time in the past Porridge Hall had been divided into two, and one half sold off. By the time it came to Robin's mother it was patched and shabby and people said it was called Porridge Hall because that was all its inhabitants could afford to eat.

"Which is very nearly true," admitted Mrs. Brogan. She painted the window frames, changed its name to Sea View, and attempted to restore the family fortunes by running it as a bed-and-breakfast business.

"If I ever start behaving like a bed and breakfaster," said Mrs. Brogan after one particularly unpleasant visitation, "break it to me gently, Robin, and I will do the decent thing and fling myself off the cliffs."

"Bed and breakfasters never do the decent thing," Robin pointed out, "but if you *do* get like them I will probably fling you off myself. Only you usually say they're not that bad."

"Hmm," said Mrs. Brogan. "Well, they usually pay before they leave; it makes all the difference. We shall never get rich at this rate."

It did not seem very likely. Although they both worked very hard and most bed and breakfasters paid their bills instead of sneaking off in the early morning and leaving no address, as fast as the money came in tiles fell off the roof or the car broke down and needed expensive repairs. Nevertheless they kept trying to manage. The beach was straight across the road and the cliffs were golden red on either side and the garden was beautiful. Robin had lived there for all of his ten years and never wanted to live anywhere else.

"Glad to be coming home?" asked his mother as they drove back from the hospital.

"Very," said Robin. "Have we got anyone staying?"

"No. We had an awful pair last night though. They came down complaining that the hot water had run out. 'I bet you don't have two baths each a day with the water right up to your necks at home!' I told them. They went off in a huff. And they picked a bunch of tulips for themselves before they left! My beautiful tulips! I could cheerfully have strangled them! Cheerfully! What are you grinning about?"

"Nothing."

"It's no joke trying to grow tulips in the winds we get here! Oh well, here we are! Macaroni and cheese for supper!"

"Good," said Robin, and then they were home. He saw immediately that the "No Vacancies" sign was up, which always happened on special occasions. He also noticed that the line that read, "Well-trained dogs welcome" had been painted out. Mrs. Brogan saw him looking but she only said, "How's that arm?"

"Fine," said Robin, which was not quite true, but he was so grateful that well-trained dogs were no longer welcome that he did not feel like complaining.

The bump on Robin's head soon disappeared but the stitches were magnificent. Twenty-four in bright blue thread. They cheered up the start of school tremendously. Nobody in the class had ever seen anything quite so gruesome—not, so to speak, in the flesh. Robin's stitches were very much in the flesh; they were in his left arm and looked terrible. Even after they were taken out there were still the scars and they were nearly as bad.

"How many did he have?" they asked each other at school.

"Dozens. About forty. All in knots."

"Tell me again what happened to your head, Robin!"

"It got banged," said Robin, who hated fuss.

"It hit a rock! He got concussion! He blacked out for three days!"

"I didn't!" protested Robin.

"It could have damaged his brain!"

"What brain?" asked Dan, and was ignored.

"Let's see the scar!"

Robin explained that there was no scar, but he was quickly overruled. They found a line on his head where the hair grew in the wrong direction.

"That's where his head split open!"

"What happened to the dog? Was it put to sleep?"

"I don't know," said Robin. "I hope not. I don't think it was. It was my fault for running and pulling away when it grabbed my arm. Half my fault anyway." He spoke bravely, but the memory still frightened him very much. He did not like to talk about it, but the class could not hear enough. Dan, their former hero, was utterly disregarded. The previous term he had distinguished himself by being rushed to the hospital in an ambulance after having collapsed (screaming) during afternoon school. Appendicitis brought on by too much lunch was the unofficial diagnosis, and for a time stomachaches had been the fashion. Dan was often called on in a medical capacity to judge the severity of his classmates' pains and he derived enormous pleasure from describing his own agonies. Now it was all over, and dog bites and blue thread stitches were wasted on Robin. He merely showed his arm and stated the facts. The rest of the class (except for the scoffing and demoted Dan) were left to supply the drama. They did it beautifully.

"A great big dog got him," went the story around the school.

"Eighty stitches in his arm!"

"Nearly ripped it off!"

"His head was split open!"

"Right open!"

"They took him in an ambulance! He blacked out for days! Everyone saw the stitches! Bright blue thread in knots!"

The story grew and grew, the stitches multiplied, and the bump on Robin's head became a fractured skull. The whole class grew more or less afraid of dogs and the few people who had them at home as pets kept quiet about the matter. Owning a dog became a shameful thing. Anyone in any doubt only had to look at Robin's arm to see the truth of that.

This state of affairs continued until spring vacation. Dan had never liked Robin—they were beachcombing rivals for one thing—and Dan had always resented the fact that Robin had never acknowledged his leadership. Now he became Robin's enemy, a lonely and self-imposed position that he did not enjoy.

"Boasting because a dog bit you!" he taunted Robin.

"I don't!"

"Getting everyone trailing after you!"

"Well, they trailed after you when you had your appendix out! I can't stop them! They just do it! I don't want them to!"

In Dan's opinion that just made it worse. He had loved being trailed after and he missed his audience very much.

"Woof, woof! Scared of dogs!" jeered Dan. His conversations with Robin always ended with this remark. Robin could never think of a suitable reply.

It was no fun being scared of dogs. It was a great nuisance, and embarrassing too. Very embarrassing sometimes, especially when his mother saw him jump out of his skin at the sound of a fat corgi panting at a garden gate.

"Look, Robin," she said, "there are dogs in the world. You have to face it."

"I know," said Robin.

"Well then. You don't have to like them. You just have to cope with them."

"I know," said Robin again.

"You panic before you think," said his mother.

"It's their breathing," said Robin, "you know, when they puff!"

Mrs. Brogan did not seem to think this was a reasonable explanation. She kept saying, "Dogs breathe, Robin! They do! They have to! And they know when someone's frightened of them and it makes them worse."

"Everyone in my class is afraid of dogs," said Robin. "Except Dan."

"Rubbish," said his mother. Her temper was always very short as summer approached and the holiday season got underway. "Dan's the only one of you with any sense then! I always said he wasn't all bad! And the rest are just frightened because it's the fashion to be frightened!"

"They're scared stiff," said Robin, but his mother was right.

Halfway through the next term everything changed. The house next door to the Brogans' that had stood empty for nearly a year suddenly was sold and a family moved in.

"Twins just your age," Mrs. Brogan reported. "A girl and a boy, and another boy a bit younger and a little girl of six. I've been talking to their mother. The twins will be in your class; I said was it worth starting them for just a few weeks but she wants them out from under her feet."

Mrs. Brogan was delighted at the thought of children coming to live next door. For the past two years, ever since the car crash that had killed his father, she had watched Robin become more and more lonely. She did not know why, because she did not realize that at the time Robin's class teacher had warned the class:

"I don't want to hear of any of you pestering Robin with questions about his father or the accident. Leave him in peace when he comes back."

Robin's class had done just that, but because it was astonishingly difficult to avoid the subjects of fathers and cars forever, they had got into the habit of avoiding Robin instead. If Robin noticed he said nothing about it.

* * *

The rivalry between Dan and Robin was at its worst when the twins appeared on the scene. It was a custom in the school to encourage different pupils to give a short talk to their schoolmates during morning assembly, and on the twins' first morning Dan had volunteered to do the honors. With a lot of help from his astonished teacher he had prepared a sermon on Lost Property. As soon as the principal had finished welcoming the twins and the gasps of horror at their names had died away, he jumped to his feet and marched on to the stage.

"Class 4A," he said, "are a bunch of drips! They go trailing round after Robin Brogan just because he had a few stitches in his arm! They're all scared of dogs all of a sudden! My mum says the whole pack of them hasn't got two brain cells to rub together and if those two new ones with the funny names don't stop laughing . . ."

"DANIEL, OUT!" roared the principal. "OUTSIDE AT ONCE! Wait outside my room!"

"I'm only saying what I think!" said Dan, retreating to the door.

"OUT!" repeated the principal, "and everybody stand! We will now sing *Summer Suns Are Glowing*, and, reluctant as I am to ask new pupils to leave the room on their first day with us, if the Robinson twins cannot control themselves they had better join Daniel! Thank you, Mrs. James!"

Mrs. James struck up the opening notes, the school stood up and sang, and Peregrine and Antoinette Robinson, still giggling uncontrollably, staggered out of the room and bumped into Dan, who was having second thoughts about the wisdom of his sermon.

"We've been sent out," said the twin who had been introduced as Peregrine. "Do you always have brilliant assemblies like that?"

"Mind your own business," said Dan, who made enemies as naturally as he breathed.

"They were boring as boring at our old school," said his twin. "We'd have got half killed if we'd done anything like that."

"Oh, shut up," said Dan, strongly suspecting he was about to get half killed himself and not liking the reminder. "Why have you got such stupid names?"

"Our mum and dad picked them."

"They must be nuts then! Peregrine and Antoinette!"

"They are nuts," agreed a twin tranquilly. "They called us after our grandparents. I don't know why they wanted to. Everyone just calls us Perry and Ant though. I'm Perry and she's Ant."

"Just as bad!"

"We know," agreed Ant. "We've got used to it though."

"Perry's a bit like Danny," suggested Perry.

"It isn't!" replied Dan furiously. "And nobody calls me Danny! And I think you're a pair of giggling drips like the rest of 4A!"

"Oh well," said Perry, "you don't even know us, so what does it matter?"

Dan glared at them. Even in class 4A he had never met people so hard to antagonize.

"You've got a brother at this school, haven't you?" he demanded.

"What about him?" asked Perry, suddenly cautious.

"He's bats," said Dan. "We've been told to be nice to him."

This time he struck gold.

"Two against one is never fair," said the principal some time later, "and if you don't want to explain your actions I can only assume that you are ashamed of them."

Perry and Ant stared gloomily at the carpet of the principal's office and said nothing.

"You had better apologize to Dan and go back to your class."

"Sorry," said Perry and Ant, still gazing at the carpet.

"Daniel?"

"What?" said Dan.

"I presume you accept their apology and are very sorry for your part in it all?"

"Who? Me?" asked Dan, outraged.

"Good," said the principal, opening the door for the twins and watching them disappear down the corridor. "Now you and I will have a chat, Daniel. Are you sitting comfortably? Then I'll begin!"

Perry and Ant continued to cause sensation. Being twins seemed to give them twice the confidence of ordinary new pupils. If their stomachs quailed at the thought of starting a new school halfway through the term they did not show it. On the first morning their mother had taken them to the school gates, but on the second day they marched boldly into the playground alone. Not quite unaccompanied, however, because after them followed their dog.

Class 4A fled wailing to their classroom, but the twins did not appear until much later.

"Where's your dog?" demanded someone at recess.

"We had to take him back home. That's why we were late."

"Is he savage?"

"'Course he's not!"

"All the ones round here are! You should see Robin Brogan's arm!"

Dan, overhearing this remark, sniffed scornfully and turned away.

"What's the matter with it?" demanded Perry, and, "What am I looking for?" asked Ant when Robin had been badgered into rolling up his sleeve.

"Look at those scars!"

But unfortunately the scars had already faded. Robin's arm had to be twisted and turned to catch the light before they really showed.

"That's where the dog got him last Easter!"

"Does it still hurt?" asked Ant.

"No," said Robin.

"He had to go to the hospital! His head was split right open! Look at the way his hair grows sideways! His arm was nearly ripped off! They sewed it back together with bright blue thread!"

"Funny," remarked Perry, "how they always stitch you up with bright blue thread. They did my leg when I fell down a drain!"

"Down a drain?"

"Yes," agreed Ant, "and they did my hand when it went through the kitchen window, but they used black on our brother when he fell off my bike."

"What color did they use on Beany's eye?"

"Bright blue," Perry reminded her. "It looked awful."

Class 4A listened in amazement to this casual account of family patchwork.

"Have you all been stitched up?"

"Haven't you?" asked Perry, surprised. "It's not that bad. You get used to it. Even Old Blanket's had stitches. He got stuck in barbed wire."

"Who's Old Blanket?"

"Our dog. He came this morning and you all ran off."

"Why do you call him Old Blanket?" asked Robin.

"It's short for Old Ironing Blanket. It's what Beany called him when she was little."

"Is Beany your sister? Why'd you call her Beany?"

"She used to want to be a bean."

"A baked bean?"

"A broad bean," explained Ant patiently. "Why'd they call you Robin?"

"I was born at Christmas," said Robin.

"They should have called you Crackers," said Perry, and fell over laughing.

It was the beginning of the end. The next morning Old Blanket came to school again, trailing a length of chewed string. Mrs. Robinson was summoned to collect him, but before she got there Old Blanket had begged for potato chips, rolled over and died, dribbled a football around the playground, and stood patiently while Perry and Ant pushed their bare hands into his mouth to prove that he did not bite. He had also shaken hands with the entire class except Robin and Dan, and Class 4A were now devoted dog lovers. It was noticeable that those who had been the loudest screamers were now the most ardent worshippers. Robin retreated to the school porch, where he discovered Dan drawing unflattering pictures of his schoolmates on the wall.

"Woof, woof," said Dan.

"Oh, shut up!" said Robin.

By the end of the term the twins were enormously popular. The class vied for their admiration, becoming more and more daring and demanding blue thread stitches for every cut and scrape. Public opinion turned against Robin. Nobody could understand why he did not like dogs. As school drew to a close his stitches diminished in number and his hair was discovered to grow no more sideways than anyone else's.

"I never said it did," said Robin, but nobody took any notice. He was no longer the center of attention. He did not mind this; unlike Dan, he had never enjoyed it, but he did wish the twins knew the facts of the matter. Although they never said anything, it was perfectly obvious that they thought him a nonentity. They steered clear of Dan altogether, except when Dan was so pugnacious they were forced to notice him.

Despite the coolness between the twins and Robin, the Porridge Hall families became friends, or at least their parents did. Mrs. Brogan and Mrs. Robinson visited each other and worried about their children together, and six-year-old Beany took to popping in next door to chat with Mrs. Brogan. She was fascinated with the bed-and-breakfast trade and begged her mother to join Mrs. Brogan in plying it.

"Don't be silly!" said Mrs. Robinson laughing. "Anyway, we haven't the space."

"I could sleep in the shed," offered Beany, "or a tent in the garden." But Mrs. Robinson was not tempted and Mrs. Brogan said she was quite right.

"Don't you like bed and breakfasters?" asked Beany.

"Some of them are very nice," replied Mrs. Brogan cautiously, "but on the whole they are such a peely-wally lot! Always wanting coat hangers and hot water and televisions! Not that I begrudge them coat hangers, except when they take them away! And I wish they would stay more than a day or two. I get tired of putting on clean sheets every day for a different lot of people!"

"Clean sheets every day!" exclaimed Beany. "Why don't you just smooth the old ones out?"

"If my customers hear you talking like that business will be even worse," Mrs. Brogan told her.

"Is business bad?" asked Beany.

"Quite bad," said Mrs. Brogan.

"Is that why your house is falling to pieces?" asked Beany. She possessed a terrible honesty for which her mother apologized.

"Oh, don't worry," replied Mrs. Brogan. "She's quite right, the house *is* falling to pieces! Anyway, I'm getting fond of Beany. She came round last night to show us a bean!"

"Look!" Beany had said, popping open a broad bean pod to show the cool fat beans inside, each in its own white bean-shaped nest. "Wouldn't you like to be one?"

"Too squashed for me," said Robin, although secretly he couldn't help thinking that Beany had a point. It looked a comfortable life, being a bean. Robin's own life seemed to grow less comfortable every day.

Dan had begun to waylay him on the way home, shoving and taunting and barking like a dog. The twins knew nothing of this until the last day of term, when they came across Dan holding Robin at bay against a holly tree, having stolen his school report. Dan was twice the size of either Robin or the twins and they hesitated for a moment before rushing to the rescue, and in that moment Robin, losing patience at last, shot out a thin brown arm and punched Dan hard on the nose.

"I'm calling the police," yelled Dan, doubled over and pouring bright red blood. "I'm calling the police and I'm telling my mum!"

The twins regarded him with interest.

"It comes out even faster when you shout," said Ant.

"You're not really calling the police, are you?" asked Perry. "They might laugh."

"I ought to," said Dan, mopping his nose with Robin's report.

"Put your head between your legs," advised Robin. "That's what you do for nosebleeds."

"You dry up!" said Dan.

"You do look funny," remarked Perry, "holding your nose like that as if it was going to drop off."

"'Tisn't funny at all," said Dan, "and if someone gave me something to mop it with I'd be able to let go."

Ant fished in her pocket and produced a grubby piece of tissue, which she handed to Dan.

"S'got blood on already," he complained ungratefully.

"Not human," said Ant reassuringly.

"I bet it's your kid brother's then," said Dan. "They send kids like him to special schools." And he grinned gorily into the twins' furious faces, screwed up Robin's report, hurled it into the holly tree, and ran off down the road before any of them could do anything about it.

two
● ● ● ● ●

"What started it?" asked Perry, as Dan disappeared.

"Nothing much." Robin dropped down from the holly tree very scratched and red but holding his report. "He was just going on and on about being scared of dogs as usual."

"Does he do that often then?" asked Ant. "We'd have come and rescued you if we'd known."

"I don't need rescuing," said Robin. "And I'm not scared of dogs; or anyway, I soon won't be. I've been training myself not to be. And I never was scared of Dan."

"No," agreed Perry, as if there had never been any question about that. Robin's single devastating punch had been a huge revelation to the twins. He had risen enormously in their estimation. Perry, the optimist of the two, was feeling very pleased with himself. He had argued all along that Robin had possibilities but Ant had always disagreed.

"I thought you were soft and stuck up and scared of

dogs," she told Robin, intending no offense at all.

"Ant!" groaned Perry.

"But Perry didn't think you were. We've been wondering about you for ages!"

Robin suddenly grinned, recognizing that Ant was one of those rare people who could not help stating the truth.

"We never hear you through the walls when we're at home. Our next-door neighbors where we lived before used to complain all the time," continued Ant. "They said they could hear us fighting through our walls."

"I heard screaming a couple of nights ago," Robin replied. "I hear it quite often, actually. Not fighting though."

"That's our brother," said Ant gloomily, "having nightmares."

"Oh," said Robin, but he added presently, "Dan's got it in for your brother. I'd tell him to keep out of his way if I were you. He's a bit odd, Dan is, sometimes."

"So's our brother," said Ant. "It's no good telling him anything."

"He did go to a special school once," Perry added. "It was one for extra clever children, but he's better now."

"He's not," said Ant.

"I mean he turned out not to be extra clever," explained Perry. "He's still just as crazy."

"Look!" exclaimed Ant suddenly. "I can see our mums looking to see why we've taken so long."

Sure enough, far down the road Mrs. Brogan and Mrs. Robinson were hanging over their garden gates and waving to their offspring.

"We thought you must be together," said Mrs.

Robinson as the twins charged up to her. "Have you been fighting?"

"Looks horribly like it," remarked Mrs. Brogan, recoiling in disgust from Robin's report. "Whose blood is this?"

"Only Dan's," answered Robin.

"Robin bashed him," Perry told her.

"I don't like fistfights," said Mrs. Brogan. "What happened to Dan? Is he all right?"

"He ran off," said Robin. "It was only one punch; you couldn't really call it a fight."

"Glad to hear it," replied his mother. "Especially as I like Dan! He's not half as bad as most people say!"

"That's not what I've heard," said Mrs. Robinson.

"Well, he's bad tempered," agreed Mrs. Brogan, "and a bit of a bully, and he bears grudges terribly, but apart from that . . . and he can be very rude, I suppose . . . what are you all laughing at?"

"Oh, nothing," said Mrs. Robinson. "Now then, you two ragamuffins! Get inside and clean yourselves up a bit! Mrs. Brogan has invited you to supper."

"All of us or just me and Ant?" asked Perry.

"All of you," said Mrs. Brogan. "We thought it was about time you made friends, but don't bother getting too clean. Come as you are! We're not proud!"

"I am," said Mrs. Robinson, and herded the twins indoors. They reappeared some time later, looking much cleaner and bringing with them Beany and their eight-year-old brother.

"Sun Dance!" said Perry, introducing him. "Because we used to play Butch Cassidy and the Sun Dance Kid! I was Butch and Ant was Cassidy. It was ages ago but everyone still calls him Sun Dance."

Sun Dance was small and dark with round reflecting glasses. In a quick husky voice he informed Robin and Mrs. Brogan that he was allergic to bread and butter and was only allowed to wash his hands once a day because he had just come out of the hospital.

"I fell under a train," he said as he politely shook hands with Mrs. Brogan. "I had to grab its wheels to stop it! I thought I saw someone trying to burgle your house this morning. Our dog's a killer but I'm not scared of him!"

It was impossible not to like Sun Dance; he was so terribly anxious to please. He had forgotten his name, was constantly distracted by the world around him, and had never been in any other state but lost. The twins felt continually obliged to explain him.

"He reads things," said Ant, as if that accounted for Sun Dance's worst flights of imagination, "and they get into his head and stick there, don't they, Sun Dance?"

"My head is too full," agreed Sun Dance. "I think Perry's and Ant's are nearly empty."

The twins did not contradict him. Compared to Sun Dance, they realized, their heads were empty. Beany had another story. She thought that what Sun Dance needed was a twin to talk to.

"Perry has Ant and Ant has Perry and I have Colin my twin cat, he was born on the same day as me, but Sun Dance hasn't got anyone."

"I've got Sun Dance," said Sun Dance. "He's here now. He's sitting on the stairs eating his football boots.

There's burglars all over. I read about them in the paper."

"Oh, Sun Dance!" said Ant, embarrassed, but Mrs. Brogan asked no questions. She had already heard a great deal about Sun Dance from Mrs. Robinson and she just laughed and said there was no need for anyone to eat football boots and sat them all down to supper. Afterward she and Sun Dance did the bed-and-breakfast accounts and she discovered that Sun Dance could add and subtract and multiply in his head as fast as Mrs. Brogan's calculator.

"He's got a gift," she said to Sun Dance's father a few days later.

"More like a curse," replied Mr. Robinson, who knew that his son's thoughts flickered through his brain like changing pictures on a television screen. "More like a curse! He has a bad time with some people. Your Robin's been very good to him."

At Mrs. Brogan's suggestion the boys had gone beachcombing the next day.

"Beachcombing?" asked Perry, who had never heard the word before.

"Treasure hunting along the tideline," Mrs. Brogan explained. "It's surprising what you can find."

"Can you keep it?" asked Ant.

"As far as I know you can," replied Mrs. Brogan. "There's ancient laws about beachcombing."

"Ancient laws," repeated Sun Dance dreamily. He and Beany went with the twins but quickly became bored and drifted away until they came across Dan, who was indulging in his usual summer occupation of looking for trouble. Sun Dance made the mistake of trying to confide his thoughts to Dan.

"Liar, liar, liar!" jeered Dan, so Sun Dance flew into a terrible rage and bit him. By the time Beany's screams had summoned Robin and the twins, Sun Dance was being held in a ferocious arm lock.

"Let him go!" they shouted, but Dan would not let go and Robin, most reluctantly, was forced to bloody his nose once again.

"Why'd you keep doing that?" bawled Dan.

"There's ancient laws!" yelled Sun Dance. "Ancient laws! Ancient laws! Let me go and I'll bite him again."

"Don't be crazy," said Ant, hanging on to Sun Dance as he lunged forward.

"He should be locked up," said Dan.

"Go tell your mum," said Robin.

"Robin's brave," said Sun Dance that night and the twins nodded in agreement. Dan stood head and shoulders above anyone else in 4A, and even the hotheaded and optimistic Perry hesitated before tackling him. He and Ant had been relieved that their share in the morning's violence had consisted only of frog-marching Sun Dance home. They were so grateful to Robin that they offered to cure his fear of dogs.

"I'm curing myself," said Robin.

"How?" demanded Perry.

"I get dog books out of the library," explained Robin (rather reluctantly because his method of curing himself was not working very well), "and read about how clever they are and about them saving people's lives and things."

"That's no good," said Ant. "You need real dogs!"

"Your way will take forever," said Perry. "You'd better come with us. It'll only take a morning!"

"You hope!" said Robin skeptically, but nevertheless he agreed to go with them. They took him on a carefully devised walk that began with a poodle that stared wistfully through a lace-curtained window, past a labrador sleeping in a car, a distant collie in a garden, a boxer on a chain, and the vicar's guide dog, who was allowed in church and who, said some unkind people, always looked far more respectable than the vicar. The walk culminated in the corgi at the gate, and although by sheer willpower they managed to get Robin past they could not get him back again and had to go a mile out of their way to get home.

"I thought we'd done it till we got to that rotten corgi!" said Ant.

"Sorry," said Robin, also depressed.

"You ought to start with Old Blanket," said Perry. "He's as tame as a mouse. Or are you scared of mice?"

"'Course not," answered Robin.

"Cows, cats, horses, elephants, lions?" asked Ant.

"I don't think so," said Robin. "I wasn't when we went to the zoo at half-term. I was just sorry for them."

"Were you scared," asked Perry cunningly, "of the wolves at the zoo?"

"Yes," said Robin.

"Oh," said the twins, disappointed, and gave it up. Robin thought they had abandoned him as a hopeless cause until Perry came searching for him that afternoon.

"If you're not scared of tigers come outside and look over the wall into our garden. I'll come with you. It's quite safe."

Intrigued, Robin followed Perry into the garden, climbed up his side of the wall, and looked out onto the Robinsons' lawn. Old Blanket, looking more like an old ironing blanket than ever, was lying in the middle of it wearing Perry and Ant's black-and-yellow striped football socks pulled as high up as they would go on each leg. He was keeping very still so as not to spill the paint water that Beany had balanced by his ear. Beany had her paint box beside her and had just finished painting black stripes across his dingy brown back.

"I've nearly finished," Beany told them as she sloshed black rings around Old Blanket's tail and completed the job by dipping the end in her paint pot. "Doesn't he look brilliant?"

"He doesn't look much like a tiger," said Perry. "He doesn't look much like anything. Poor Old Blanket. Come here!"

Old Blanket heaved himself to his feet, padded over, and stood wagging his tail apologetically.

"How could anyone be afraid of that!" demanded Perry. "Look, he's too ashamed to even hold his head up!"

Old Blanket sighed and glanced miserably down at his wrinkled socks and Robin suddenly found that he was not afraid. Very cautiously he reached down a hand to touch Old Blanket.

"There!" said Perry triumphantly as Robin's hand rested for a second on Old Blanket's head. "Don't stop doing it!" he added and slid down from the wall and rushed indoors to fetch Mrs. Brogan. "I've cured him!" he announced, beaming. "Come and see quick! Robin's stroking our Old Blanket! He's stopped being scared, haven't you, Robin?"

"Fancy being afraid of Old Blanket in the first place," said Mrs. Brogan. "You might as well be afraid of a door-mat!" But she grinned encouragingly at Robin as he reached down to touch Old Blanket again.

"Old Blanket can be very fierce," Perry told her indignantly. "He could be if he had to be, I mean, only he's never needed to be yet."

"He'll have to be now he's a tiger," said Beany.

Old Blanket gave her a thoughtful look and started pulling off a sock with his teeth. When Robin bent to help him he held up one grateful paw after another until his legs were free.

"Hi! Stop it!" shouted Beany. "I'd just got him done!"

"I hope that paint isn't poisonous," remarked Mrs. Brogan as Old Blanket began licking his chest.

"It isn't," Perry replied. "It can't be because he was a leopard yesterday but he licked off all his spots in the night. Beany's playing jungles. She wants to paint me and Ant into monkeys but we're not letting her and neither will Sun Dance."

"Why ever not?" asked Mrs. Brogan. "What better way to spend an afternoon?"

"We would but we're digging up a corpse we've found behind the compost heap," explained Perry. "We've found a lot of bones down there. We're going to wire them all together when we've got them out. Dad says skeletons are worth a lot of money. But we don't know what to do with Sun Dance."

"Why not?"

"He won't be a painted monkey and Mum won't let him dig for bones in case he gets too excited. He's been walking in his sleep again."

"Poor old Sun Dance!"

"He's been wild since Dan got him. Dad found him trying to get the front door open at two o'clock this morning. He said he was going down to the beach to do the accounts. He still keeps wanting to go to the beach but he's not allowed by himself."

Robin took the hint and offered to go with him and was flattered when Mrs. Robinson agreed that he could.

"Just make sure you stay on the beach and keep away from that dangerous cliff path," she told Robin. "I'd rather he forgot that it was there."

Robin agreed, but Sun Dance was not interested in the cliff path. He wanted especially to go to the beach and grumbled frightfully when they found it deserted.

"I like it better empty," said Robin, but Sun Dance did not agree.

"There's ancient laws against bashing people up," he said. "I wanted to tell Dan!"

"You leave Dan alone," advised Robin. "He's not the sort you can tell things like that to!"

"I bet Perry and Ant haven't really found a man," said Sun Dance even more gloomily. "How would he get there in all his bones?"

"Don't know," said Robin.

"He'd have to lie down and wrap the earth round him," said Sun Dance, folding the air around himself as he spoke. "Unless someone put him there!"

"Why'd they do that?" asked Robin, startled.

"To save him from the dogs, I suppose," said Sun Dance.

"Sun Dance!" exclaimed Robin, appalled. He was glad he had thought to bring a football with them. It was an old, slightly soft one that he had found earlier in the year but it temporarily distracted Sun Dance. They kicked it between them, running along the edge of the waves where the sand was hard.

"When is it a goal?" asked Sun Dance.

"When it goes into the sea," said Robin, and they got wetter and wetter saving each other's goals until the ball floated too far out to sea to be retrieved.

"Will the waves wash it back again?" asked Sun Dance.

"Not now," said Robin. "The tide's just turned. It might easily come back at high tide tomorrow, though. I'll come down in the morning and have a look."

Sun Dance, who had been cheerful all the time they had been playing football, suddenly remembered the twins again.

"What if they've found its head?"

"Who?"

"Perry and Ant."

"It's not really a person, Sun Dance," Robin said. "You said yourself it couldn't be. Perry and Ant just like pretending it is. I bet it's just a heap of old bones that some dog buried a long time ago."

"Heads are full of brains," said Sun Dance, uncomforted. "Raw brains! Warm raw brains! What came out of Dan's nose when you hit him?"

"A little bit of blood," said Robin. "Anyway, forget

about brains! Let's go back along the tideline and see what we can find."

"There won't be anything," said Sun Dance, still miserable.

"There might be! There nearly always is. That's why they made the ancient laws my mum told you about. I can see something already!"

"Where?" asked Sun Dance.

"There! That black heap on the tideline. Race you to it!"

Sun Dance, who had smiled at the mention of his beloved ancient laws, began running, and Robin, very relieved to leave the subject of raw warm brains, followed after him. As they drew closer to the black heap he suddenly stopped. It had moved. Sun Dance, who had been twitchy with nerves all afternoon, saw it at the same time, jerked to a halt, and caught Robin's arm. A moment later the black heap moved again, shook its head, and staggered to its feet. As fast as it could it scuttled away.

"It's a dog!" announced Sun Dance, greatly relieved because he had thought it was somehow Ant and Perry's man. "It's a poor little dog! You're not frightened, are you?"

"No," said Robin, and he thought triumphantly that that was two dogs in one day that he had not been frightened of. "No, I'm not, but it's scared of us, I think." And he looked regretfully after the little dog. It was far in the distance, no longer running but searching among the washed up seaweed and rubbish.

"I think he's looking for something to eat," said Sun Dance.

"Perhaps he just likes the smells."

"He's hurt his leg. He's hopping."

"He's probably all right," said Robin reassuringly. "Having an afternoon out. It's time we were going home, Sun Dance."

"Where will he go to?" asked Sun Dance, following reluctantly.

"Back to where he lives, I suppose."

"He's lying down again," said Sun Dance, turning around after a little while to squint against the sunshine. "He's lost!"

"Well, someone will come and find him."

"If they don't, do you know what?" asked Sun Dance. "He'll be yours! You found him! Ancient laws! Like your mum said!"

"You and your ancient laws!" said Robin, but Sun Dance tore home chanting the words over and over again while the sun danced on his spectacles and Robin ran breathless behind him.

Perry and Ant met them at the garden gate. They were almost entirely covered in mud, and had laid out, as a welcome to the travelers, a man in bones upon the front lawn.

"What d'you think?" demanded Ant proudly.

They had spaced the bones out as far as possible but even so the man looked very short. Suspiciously short. Also, Mrs. Brogan and Mrs. Robinson were standing together in the front porch doubled over with laughter. They did not seem to think that Sun Dance would be alarmed and Sun Dance was not.

"He's all made out of the same sort of bones!" he announced after one glance. "Chop bones!"

Perry and Ant stared at him in amazement.

Although they had already heard this sad fact from their mother it was very disconcerting to hear it repeated again by Sun Dance.

"Chop Bone Man!" continued Sun Dance cheerfully. "That's what you've found! He needs a proper head. Guess who scored the most goals!"

"You!" said Mrs. Brogan.

"Wrong," said Sun Dance happily. "Robin did! It was eleven—six and then the ball floated away, but it's coming back tomorrow and Robin's got a dog. Ancient laws! And it was only blood came out of Dan's nose. Not brains. He wasn't there, though."

"So you had a good afternoon?" asked Mrs. Robinson.

"Very," said Sun Dance.

three
● ● ● ● ● ● ●

That night Robin dreamed of dogs. It was the same old chasing dream that he had had on and off since Easter but this time, just before he woke up, it changed. The dog that had been behind him was suddenly in front, far in the distance, moving slowly, and then more slowly across the sands. It turned into the dog that he and Sun Dance had discovered and Robin woke up remembering it and hoping it had been found.

He had slept late. There were none of the usual sounds of getting up from next door, and downstairs he could hear his mother singing as she cooked the bed and breakfasters their breakfasts. Robin hurried down to help but found he was not needed.

"Slimming vegetarians," explained his mother. "Very nice people too! 'You are what you eat,' I told them and they entirely agreed so they're having brown toast and orange juice. I offered to cook them scrambled eggs and kippers so my conscience is free."

"Thought you sounded cheerful," commented Robin.

"Doesn't take much to raise my spirits," agreed Mrs. Brogan. "A day off bacon and sausages goes to my head like strong drink and money! What are you planning to do this morning?"

"I'm going to look for my football," Robin told her, "just in case it came back with the last tide. Perhaps the twins and Sun Dance will come and help."

However, when he went to look for his neighbors he found the house deserted. The only person at home was Chop Bone Man, still spread-eagle on the front lawn. Robin suddenly remembered that Mrs. Robinson had threatened to take her family shopping if she could get them up early enough.

"Big shopping?" Beany had asked in horror, and Mrs. Robinson had said yes. Big shopping was done in the nearest large town, fifteen miles away, a place Mrs. Brogan and Mrs. Robinson thought of wistfully now and then. Its department stores, huge library, and decent hairdressers lured them back to its gritty charms every month or so. Their children detested it and as Robin crossed the road to the beach he felt a warm feeling of happiness inside himself, simply because he was not there.

He found his football almost immediately but it was in a completely inaccessible place. Dan was sitting on it. That was perfectly fair; weeks earlier Robin had found it washed up on the beach and had kept it and now Dan had done the same. Robin would have taken no notice if it had not been for the expression on Dan's face. He looked as if he was in great pain.

"Are you all right?" he asked.

Dan made no reply but clutched his ears and looked anguished.

"You look awful," said Robin, genuinely alarmed. "Really ill! I'll go and get my mother."

"Don't be stupid," replied Dan crossly, "I was trying to think."

To prove it he let go of his ears and recited:

"'Robin Brogan and his friend
Is completely round the bend!'

"It should be 'friends' though," he added, "because those twins are as cracked as that kid brother of theirs . . . Where is your nutty little friend?"

"Sitting on a football," said Robin.

"Very funny," said Dan, getting up off the football and balancing it neatly on one finger. "You know who I mean! Two of a kind, you and him!"

"Good," said Robin.

"Woof, woof," said Dan disagreeably. "I'd run off home if I were you! This beach is a dangerous place! There's a dead dog lying back along there waiting to get you!"

"Dead!" exclaimed Robin, horrified. "How do you know?"

"Saw it when I found this," said Dan, kicking the ball upwards and bouncing it on his head.

"What did it die of?"

"How should I know?" demanded Dan between bumps. "It's miles back. Drowned probably. I didn't go right up to it. Guess where I went last night?"

"Bed," said Robin, staring down the beach.

"Doctor's," said Dan. "My mum took me to show him my nose. He said I ought to stop getting it thumped."

Robin continued to stare vacantly along the beach and Dan marched away in a huff, annoyed that his visit to the medical profession had not caused the alarm he had hoped for. When he turned back to see if Robin had started worrying yet there was no one in sight.

It took a long time to find the dog. As Dan had said, it was very far along, ages past where most beachcombers gave up and turned back, but eventually Robin spotted a black heap of fur lying high up on the tideline, close under the cliffs. Only its tail sticking out showed that it was a dog at all. Very cautiously Robin went up to it and touched it with a toe and a moment later nearly jumped out of his skin as its tail lifted in a brief flicker of a wag.

Robin retreated a few steps and waited to see what would happen next. Nothing happened. He touched the dog again but it did not move and with his heart hammering rather hard he bent down and listened. He could hear no breathing. Perhaps he had imagined the wag. Very gently he passed his hand lightly over the small black head and relief flooded over him when the dog moved again.

It seemed to revive as Robin stroked it. Its eyes opened and its tail trembled, but it made no attempt to get up and underneath the thick black fur Robin could feel every bone of its ribs and backbone.

"You can't stay here," said Robin worriedly, and

rather tentatively he put an arm under the dog's chest and heaved it upright. Despite its thinness it was very heavy and as soon as Robin let go it slipped back down again. Robin decided food was the most important thing and since he could not carry the dog to food he must bring food to the dog, and the sooner the better because it looked as if it might die at any moment.

"Wait here," he commanded, and pulling off his jacket tucked it carefully around the thin black back.

"That's to prove you're mine if anyone comes," he told the dog.

Once again the tail moved, a wag of understanding.

"Don't die!" said Robin desperately, and turned and sprinted home.

Much to Robin's disappointment, the Robinsons were still away. He turned in to his own house and found his mother talking in her bed-and-breakfast voice, a more polished and nervous one than she used for every day. She caught sight of Robin and waved him to pass her a pen and shut up. When he tried to speak she drew a straight line with her finger across her throat and glared at him.

"Children are always very welcome," she said, motioning Robin to go away. This reply seemed not to please the caller. Robin saw his mother cast her eyes up to the ceiling as she replied, "No, don't worry. There are none here at present except my own son and he's very quiet! Almost self-sufficient!" she added desperately, because business really had been very bad that summer. "We hardly see him at all!"

Robin took the hint and left. In the kitchen he helped himself to a pint of milk and a package of ginger cookies. Rummaging through the cupboards he found two cans of sardines and a tub of cheese spread. He pushed everything into a bag, hurried out of the back door, and a moment later bumped straight into the twins and Sun Dance. Sun Dance was looking very sulky and Ant was looking harassed, but Perry was his usual cheerful self.

"Thought you'd gone shopping," said Robin.

"We did but Mum put us on a bus and sent us home," Perry told him happily.

"She's in an awful mood," said Ant.

"She said we were a nightmare and it would be much quicker without us," Perry explained. "Where are you going in such a rush?"

"Beach," said Robin, running and walking and then running again when he got his breath back.

"We've had a terrible morning," said Ant, panting to keep up. "Perry dropped a dozen eggs in the library!"

"Eggs!" exclaimed Robin. "I wish I'd thought of eggs!"

"They broke all over," continued Ant. "Not when he dropped them, though. Only one broke then, but a librarian came rushing over and she stepped on a lot more . . ."

"And she stepped on my hand!" put in Perry. "Without saying sorry! And Mum rushed us out so fast she left Sun Dance and the vegetables behind."

Sun Dance, who so far had not said a word, looked crosser than ever.

"They have to eat," he said.

"Not our tomatoes," said Perry.

"They have to eat *something*," said Sun Dance. "Tomatoes was all I had. You didn't give them anything."

"Hurry!" said Robin.

"*Nobody* gave them anything," continued Sun Dance. "Lucky I was there!"

"I shouldn't think a few tomatoes will help them very much," said Perry. "People can't live on tomatoes!"

"Stop arguing and come on!" said Robin.

"You haven't told us what we're running for," said Ant.

"To get to my dog," said Robin.

"Sun Dance told us you'd got a dog but we thought he was talking rubbish. He got up in the middle of the night again because he said the tide would wash it away. What's it doing on the beach?"

Robin had not breath enough to reply and the twins were still too full of the horrors of shopping to ask again.

"We lost Beany in the market," Ant related, "and then we found her by a vegetable stall popping open broad beans. Mum had to pay for them and, while she was doing it, Sun Dance started giving away tomatoes to tramps. And Beany wouldn't say she was sorry."

"Who to?" asked Robin, momentarily diverted.

"Anyone," said Ant briefly. "Why is your dog on the beach? And when did you get it? Is it all right?"

"It can't walk."

"How are you going to get it back then?" asked Perry. "Dogs are awful animals to carry. Me and Ant nearly died when we had to carry Old Blanket home last summer when he cut all his legs."

"I don't know," said Robin worriedly. "We'll have to try and carry him between us, I suppose. We could have brought Mum's wheelbarrow if I'd thought, only I don't want to go back now. I've left him too long on his own already."

"Perry and Ant'll go," announced Sun Dance, speaking for the first time.

"Would you?" asked Robin hopefully.

"Would she let us just take it?"

"No," said Robin. "She's funny about her gardening things. I lost a spade on the beach once. You'd have to sneak it away. Perhaps you'd better not."

Initially Perry and Ant had not been at all keen to be sent back, but they liked the thought of a little burglary in a good cause and volunteered to go. Robin and Sun Dance continued along the beach together and in a few moments had spotted the patch of blue that was Robin's jacket and galloped up to it. Robin saw with great relief that the dog was still alive but Sun Dance felt the knobbles of bone through the fur and began to cry.

"Poor dead dog," he sobbed, dripping tears on the sand.

"He's not dead," said Robin and ripped open the carton of milk. "He's just very hungry. Look!"

There was no bowl for the dog to drink out of but he managed to lap out of the carton. The two cans of sardines disappeared in two hungry gulps and when Robin opened the ginger cookies, Sun Dance's tears disappeared and he began to smile instead.

"What's he called?"

"I don't know," said Robin.

"He's got to have a name."

"S'pose so. But I don't know what it is."

"If he was mine I'd call him Ancient Laws," said Sun Dance, watching the dog lick cheese spread out of the tub.

Robin laughed.

"You have to call him something," persisted Sun Dance. "What about Seaweed?"

"He's not even my dog really," said Robin.

"Of course he is," said Sun Dance, astonished. "You found him. What about Cheese Face?"

"Cheese Face isn't a name," objected Robin.

Sun Dance gazed around the beach for further alternatives.

"Call him Seagull or Broken Shell."

"No."

"Cloud. Blue Patch of Sky. Rock Pool. Washed Up Dead Crab?"

"No."

"Sun Dance, after me?" suggested Sun Dance desperately. "Foot Print? Shadows On The Sand?"

"Much too long," said Robin.

"It's a pity your name isn't Robinson Crusoe," said Sun Dance.

"Why?"

"He's a dog, and it's Friday. We could have called him Dog Friday!"

"Dog Friday is brilliant!" said Robin. "Friday for short!"

By the time the twins returned, Friday was up on his feet and staggering about on three legs. They trundled him home with his tail hung backwards over one end of the wheelbarrow and his front paws hanging over the other.

"He's been dumped," said Ant. "Look! You can see where they've taken his collar off. The fur's all flat. Old Blanket was just like that when we got him from the RSPCA."

"Can I get in the wheelbarrow too?" asked Sun Dance. "For company?"

"No!" replied the pushers.

"I wonder what he is," remarked Robin. "What sort, I mean?"

"Spaniel," said Perry. "Sort of spaniel, anyway. His tail is spanielish and his ears would be if they were a bit longer and his legs would be too if they were a bit shorter . . ."

"What will your mum say?" asked Ant the realist.

"She'll say, 'Oh poor soul! It shouldn't be allowed,'" said Robin, "and then she'll start rushing round like mad trying to cure him."

"How do you know?"

"It's what she always does," explained Robin. "Hungry birds in winter, dead plants, poor people on television, even bed and breakfasters who look miserable! It's always the same. And she always says whoever's fault it is should be hung or drowned or something violent."

"Good," said Sun Dance.

"She doesn't mean it really."

Sun Dance looked very disappointed.

Mrs. Brogan fulfilled all Robin's predictions.

"Oh poor soul!" she exclaimed when they unloaded

Friday onto her kitchen floor. "I hope he's housetrained!"

"He's been dumped," Perry told her.

"It shouldn't be allowed!" said Mrs. Brogan. "They should be hung, people who do things like that! I would hang them!"

"I would help you," said Sun Dance so earnestly that Mrs. Brogan said, well, perhaps not hung.

"Drowned?" suggested Sun Dance.

"Really, Sun Dance!" she said, "but I'd like to tell them exactly what I think of them!"

While she was speaking she examined Friday's leg and bathed his paw. Then the twins were dispatched to find Old Blanket's basket that he never used (preferring beds), Robin was sent to the shop to buy dog food and Sun Dance ordered to follow him and remind him to get extra milk. Friday ate the food and drank the milk and hobbled around the kitchen exploring.

"He's changed shape after all that dinner," said Perry. "I wonder if he knows his name. Here, Friday! Come here!"

Friday pattered over to Perry, sat down and held up his sore paw to shake hands. Mrs. Robinson appeared, to inspect the new arrival.

"You've got a new lodger!" she said.

"Friday," said Sun Dance, "short for Dog Friday! He's Robin's dog now. Ancient laws and all that!"

"Someone's lost a nice little dog," said Mrs. Robinson, bending down to stroke him.

"He was being a tramp," said Sun Dance.

"Poor little thing. It shouldn't be allowed," said Mrs. Brogan. "I hate to tell the police!"

"Police!" exclaimed Robin.

"Well, he must belong to somebody!"

"But they dumped him," protested Perry. "You can see where the collar was!"

"He might have died," added Ant.

"It's still the law," said his mother. "You know it is."

"I'm very sorry, but we'll have to report him found," said Mrs. Brogan.

"Why can't we just keep him?" asked Robin, while Sun Dance shouted, "What about ancient laws? What about ancient laws? Tramps can't help it! He hasn't done anything wrong!"

"Someone might be looking for him," Mrs. Brogan pointed out, but she was ignored.

"I give them tomatoes!" said Sun Dance.

"I thought you liked him," said Robin.

"It's not a matter of liking him," replied his mother patiently. "It's doing what's right. I'm sorry, Robin. We'll tell the police that if nobody claims him we'll give him a home, but try not to count on it too much. He might have been on holiday with somebody and just strayed off."

"You said they should be hung!" said Sun Dance furiously.

"Have a heart, Sun Dance!" replied Mrs. Brogan. "If you lost Old Blanket and someone found him you'd want him back, wouldn't you?"

"Of course he would," said Mrs. Robinson, and reluctantly Robin and the twins agreed that she was right. Only Sun Dance would not be convinced and Mrs. Brogan secretly agreed with him. She found it very hard to be cheerful when the police sent down a man with a van and Friday was taken to the RSPCA kennels.

"The sooner we take him in the sooner you can have him back," the man told her. "We'll only keep him seven days."

"His paw needs seeing to and he needs feeding up," said Mrs. Brogan.

"Don't you worry," said the man cheerfully. "He'll be all right with us. I'll get someone to look at his foot and they get fed a pound of tripe a day!"

"Tripe!" repeated Mrs. Brogan when Friday had been driven away. "Poor little dog! Well, at least he's been fed properly today!"

"Yes," agreed Robin and the twins, mournfully but politely. Sun Dance was not polite.

"If I was a lost tramp would you give me to the police?" he demanded.

"No, I'd give you to your mum," said Mrs. Brogan.

Robin made a chart seven days wide and twenty-four hours deep. It was enormous. He stuck it on his bedroom wall and crossed out the hours as they passed.

"It's morbid, Robin!" said his mother when she saw it. She was worried at the thought of what would happen if someone claimed Friday, and harassed by bed and breakfasters. Four of them arrived unexpectedly late on Friday night and left on Saturday morning, taking with them eight of Mrs. Brogan's towels.

"Could they possibly have packed them by mistake?" asked Mrs. Robinson when she heard this news, but Mrs.

Brogan replied not possibly. No one could pack eight towels belonging to someone else without noticing. She added that she was tired of bed and breakfasters and wouldn't care if she never saw another one.

"Wouldn't you really?" asked Beany, who was listening.

"Not a bit!" said Mrs. Brogan, cheering up at even the thought of never having to worry about bed and breakfasters again. "Eight towels! I could strangle them!"

"You'll never get rich if you take to strangling your customers!" said Mrs. Robinson.

"Well, I might as well get a bit of job satisfaction," replied Mrs. Brogan, "since I'm never going to get rich anyway, even if I leave them all unstrangled! This has been the worst season for years!"

The cold gray summer was turning people away from seaside holidays. The telephone seemed to be constantly ringing with cancellations, and every time it rang Robin jumped out of his skin, always fearing it was the police with the news that Friday had been claimed.

"For goodness sake go out and find something to do!" Mrs. Brogan told him. "Something where you can't hear the phone!"

Robin went next door and helped the twins and Sun Dance assemble Chop Bone Man. They knotted his joints with garden twine and reinforced him with sticks filched by Perry from the vegetable patch. Dan looked over the garden wall and asked, "Dug up your granddad then?" and hurried away before anyone could think of a suitable reply.

Beany came out to inspect the remains and was not

impressed. "He needs a proper head," she said, and Ant replied that Sun Dance had insisted on going to the butcher's in the hope of acquiring one.

"Human?" asked Beany, enormously astonished.

"Pork," said Ant. "But I don't think he'll have any luck. He's been gone ages."

They were not surprised when a long time later Sun Dance returned empty-handed and weeping tears of rage.

"I told him he was a burglar," he sniffed. "'Ancient laws!' I said, but he took no notice!"

"Who? The butcher?"

"So I crept round the back and they grabbed me and put me out! I said I was only looking. They tried to act like they didn't know what I was talking about!"

"What are you talking about?" demanded Ant. "The butcher?"

"Him?" said Sun Dance. "Him? He didn't have any heads. He said they didn't have them ever. 'Animals do,' I said, 'so where do you put them?' But he wouldn't give me any so I went to the police!"

"For a head?"

"For Friday," said Sun Dance impatiently. "To claim him! They said last night that someone might turn up and claim him so I turned up!"

"Good grief!"

"'I'm a tramp,'" I said, "'and you've got my dog! He's a tramp too. I got him by ancient laws and I've come to claim him back!' But they were rotten to me!" Sun Dance sniffed self-pityingly. "So I went round the back to see if I could find him. I couldn't, though. They found me. They were very rude. 'What's your name?' they kept saying, over and over again. 'Sun Dance,' I kept telling them. I thought they were going to put me in prison! I asked them to put me in prison, with Friday, but in the end they chucked me out!"

They stared at him, speechless at his capacity to get into trouble.

"You didn't come and rescue me!" complained Sun Dance.

"We thought you'd only gone up the road to the butcher's! If Mum and Dad knew you'd been to the police station they'd never let you out again!"

"I didn't do anything wrong," replied Sun Dance crossly. "Anyway, what are you going to do about Chop Bone Man now? He just looks like string and bones without a head!"

"He is just string and bones," said Ant. "I suppose we could make him a head out of paper. Or a balloon."

"I know! Josephine!" exclaimed Beany. "You can have hers!"

With that she rushed indoors and returned a minute later with a large rag doll and her mother's sewing scissors.

"I hate Josephine!" said Beany, and chopped off her head.

No one except Robin batted an eyelid at this awful deed. He had not yet become inured to the total ruthlessness of the Robinson children. Even Ant went to extremes that Robin would never dream of. He sometimes envied them their lack of conscience. In a way they made him feel very old but then they had not had to grow up anything like as quickly as he had.

Chop Bone Man looked quite impressive with Josephine's head fixed on to his stick spine. The twins were especially proud of him. With huge generosity they offered to loan him to Robin to keep in his bedroom for company until his dog came back.

"I couldn't," said Robin reluctantly as he stood up to go home. "Mum would go mad! She's fed up enough already today."

It was this remark that inspired Beany's brilliant suggestion that Chop Bone Man should be hung in the Brogan garden, under Mrs. Brogan's bed-and-breakfast sign.

"To put the rotten bed and breakfasters off," she explained. "It's them that fed Mrs. Brogan up so much!"

The sign made a wonderful gibbet and had the advantage of being screened from the house by a lilac bush. Chop Bone Man, who really looked very nasty with his yellow stringy bones attached to Josephine's grinning head, hung beneath the sign and successfully kept off all passing trade. He was not discovered until Sunday night, when Mrs. Brogan, furious beyond belief, unfairly retraced all her rash words about never seeing a bed and breakfaster again.

"For two pins I'd string you all up beside him!" she told her neighbors.

"She doesn't mean it," said Robin.

"I do!" said Mrs. Brogan.

Only the abject apologies of the entire Robinson family appeased her. Once softened, however, she became reckless. Moved by Mrs. Robinson's wholesale condemnation of her children and a detailed account of the shopping trip, she offered to have them all stay at her house for a night while Mr. and Mrs. Robinson escaped to the bright lights.

"We couldn't possibly let you!" exclaimed Mrs. Robinson, mentally deciding what to pack.

"Of course you could," said Mrs. Brogan. "We've plenty of empty beds and it will give Robin something to think about instead of worrying about that poor little dog. He hasn't thought of anything else all weekend."

"Neither have I," said Sun Dance mournfully.

Mrs. Robinson took very little persuading. It was agreed that on Wednesday she would force her husband to take a whole day off work and they would escape together, abandoning their children for an entire day and night, during which time the abandoned children would promise to be nothing but cheerful, helpful, and polite.

"If you're sure," said Mrs. Robinson.

"Quite sure," said Mrs. Brogan. "Then there'll only be Thursday night to get through. On Friday evening Dog Friday's seven days will be up, and if all goes well we'll have him on Saturday morning. Oh Robin! And I told you not to hope too much! I'm just as bad!"

"We're really sorry about Chop Bone Man!" said Ant. "We didn't think."

"You are forgiven," said Mrs. Brogan. She went home feeling so kind and benevolent that she forgot all about the gibbet in her front garden, and Chop Bone Man hung there until well into Monday morning, continuing his good work. Eventually Ant came around and politely asked permission to collect him.

"Hell's bells and buckets of blood, Ant!" exclaimed Mrs. Brogan at this request, which Ant wisely took as consent.

four

• • • • • •

By Monday, Robin was feeling much more cheerful. The police had evidently decided to overlook Sun Dance's visit and Friday remained unclaimed. This was so encouraging that Robin raided his piggy bank and invested in a new collar and a bright red, extra long, extra strong luxury dog leash. He carried it coiled up in his jeans' pocket. Even the feel of it there was comforting. The man in the pet shop had assured him that it was the best dog leash on the market and would hold any dog, no matter how large. When he heard that it was intended for what Robin described as a sort of spaniel he suggested a much cheaper one would do just as well, but Robin would not hear of it. Where Friday was concerned only the best was good enough.

"Robin!" protested Mrs. Brogan when she saw it. "It's far too early to be buying dog leashes. Is all your money gone?"

"Nearly. There's enough for some biscuits to start him off."

"Housekeeping will pay for dog food. You needn't worry about that."

"I like buying him things," explained Robin.

"Yes, but . . . Oh well, I suppose I can't talk!"

"Why not?"

Mrs. Brogan nodded toward a box in the corner of the kitchen. "Dog food," she said. "Cans. Twenty!"

"Twenty!" repeated Robin.

"Well, if you send off twenty labels you get a free pottery bowl!"

"A dog bowl?"

"Of course a dog bowl!"

"Well then," said Robin.

"Even if we don't manage to get Friday I still think we should get a dog," replied Mrs. Brogan defensively. "So you can stop grinning at me like that! And don't say it!"

"What?"

"'I only want Friday!'" quoted Mrs. Brogan.

"All right," said Robin, "but I do."

"I know," agreed his mother. "But don't forget there are as many good fish in the sea as ever came out of it."

"There aren't dogs, though!" said Robin.

"Oh, go and buy your biscuits!" said Mrs. Brogan.

Robin went, still smiling to himself at the thought of the twenty cans of dog food.

As he came to the local shop a notice stuck among the postcards on the window caught his eye. He stopped and read it, and then read it again and again while all the happiness of the morning faded away from him.

```
LOST
BLACK SPANIEL TYPE DOG
ANSWERS TO NAME OF KEEPER
TELEPHONE: 555-6814
REWARD!
```

It could not be Friday. Whoever had taught Friday to hold up a paw to say hello had since grown tired of him. Friday had been starving and alone when Robin found him.

Perhaps his owners had changed their minds, he thought. Perhaps they had missed him after all and wished they'd kept him. Perhaps they'd started feeling guilty. It did not make sense to Robin, and whatever their reason, he decided they were too late. They had lost their right to Friday, or Keeper, as they called him. They ought not to be trusted again.

As he stared at the notice a crowd of old ladies came to the shop. They pushed through the door, gossiping and laughing, and surrounded the counter and the shop-keeper. An idea flashed into Robin's mind and a second later he was in and out of the shop, trying to look as if he had never moved, and the notice was stuffed in his pocket.

"You were very quick!" Dan appeared suddenly from nowhere and smirked as Robin jumped out of his skin.

"How do you know how long I was?"

"I was coming down the road when you went in. You were only a second!"

"I didn't buy anything."

"No, I bet you didn't," said Dan, grinning and keeping up with Robin as he walked away. "You stuffed something in your pocket, though!"

"I went to buy dog biscuits," said Robin stiffly.

"Dog biscuits!" repeated Dan skeptically. "You! Oh woof, woof!"

"I did!"

"Where are they, then? You haven't even got a dog!"

"I didn't say I had," said Robin, starting to get confused. "Anyway, I didn't buy them. Or anything. I just went in and came out."

"Oh yes?"

"Yes!"

"Fancy Robin Brogan pinching things," remarked Dan in a loud voice to nobody in particular. "Robin Brogan!"

"I didn't!"

"My mum's always telling me I should steer clear of you," continued Dan. "Wonder what she'd say if she knew!"

Robin marched down the road in silence.

"Wonder what your mum would say?" suggested Dan.

"Oh shut up!"

"Pinching things!" repeated Dan jubilantly. "If I ever pinched anything I know what would happen to me! My dad . . ." He stopped suddenly. Nobody, not even Dan at his worst, mentioned fathers to Robin. Fortunately, at that moment Sun Dance came tearing down the road to meet them.

"I've been looking for you!" he said to Dan. "I wanted to tell you what my mum said!"

"Who cares what your mum said?"

"She said I'm to stay out of your way!"

"Good!"

"Because it causes nothing but trouble trying to talk to you!"

"Who said?"

"My mum."

"Huh," said Dan.

"So I thought I'd come and tell you!"

"Push off then," said Dan.

"What?"

"Push off! Go! Clear off! Stay out of my way!"

"Who? Me?"

"Yes, you! Like your mum said!"

"Aren't you sorry?"

Dan looked at him in amazement before turning on to the path that led to the beach.

"Where are you going?"

"Mind your own business!"

"Can I come with you?" begged Sun Dance.

Dan turned and shouted something extremely rude and Robin just caught Sun Dance as he leaped to the attack.

"Let me go!" yelled Sun Dance, twisting and struggling so hard that Robin was very relieved when Mrs. Robinson came running out and towed him away.

"Thanks, Robin!" she said and then, noticing his gloomy face, "Cheer up! No harm done this time!"

Robin didn't think there was no harm done. He went up to his bedroom, and sitting with his back to the door to prevent anyone coming in unexpectedly, he ripped the notice again and again until it was reduced to a heap of feathery dust. He sat and poured it from hand to hand as he thought. His dog was being advertised for by its owners. He had been caught red-handed shoplifting by Dan. There was no imagining what Dan might do with that bit of information. For one awful moment he had thought that he was going to have to fight him again in order to shut him up. Sun Dance had arrived just in time. Poor old Sun Dance! Fleetingly it occurred to Robin that one day there would be trouble between Sun Dance and Dan, but then he started worrying about his dog again.

For the rest of that day and all of the next Robin was overwhelmed by a mixture of guilt and apprehension. He would have preferred to spend the days hovering by the telephone, waiting for the police to call with the awful news that Friday had been claimed, but the Robinson children, light-headed at the thought of a night away from their parents, constantly dragged him away to consult about their plans. This was exactly what Mrs. Brogan had hoped would happen, although she was a little startled to hear that her guests proposed to occupy the time with Murder in the Dark, pillow fights, a midnight feast, and a game called Avalanche, forbidden in their own home. It involved hurling oneself down a staircase and was perfectly safe, Ant assured Mrs. Brogan, if enough pillows and mattresses and quilts were used to cushion the descent.

Mrs. Brogan cheerfully agreed to Murder in the Dark but not the pillow fights, a midnight feast if the menu was kept within reason and plates were used, but she forbade her guests to play Avalanche at any price.

"It is a very quiet game," Beany told her earnestly. "If no one screams!"

"I would scream," said Mrs. Brogan.

Sun Dance dragged Robin off to a private corner of the garden, where he confided his plans to break into the police station and begged Robin to help.

"We could sneak off while they were playing Murder in the Dark," he said. "Easy as pie! Anyway, Friday is yours so it wouldn't count as burglaring and even if it did burglars never get caught these days, my dad says."

With the stolen notice always on his mind Robin felt in no position to judge other people's crimes, but it was obvious that Sun Dance intended to carry out his plans unless he was dissuaded.

"It would definitely count as burglaring," he told Sun Dance firmly. "And of course you'd be caught! And Mum would be furious and none of you would ever be allowed to stay again. I bet you wouldn't find Friday anyway. Even if you did and you got him home without being caught you'd be made to give him back in the morning and we'd have to start another seven days' waiting. It's a terrible idea!"

"Oh, all right," said Sun Dance cheerfully. "I'll think of something else! Do you want to help?"

Robin said that he thought Sun Dance would manage much better without him. As soon as he could he disappeared to his bedroom where he was in the process of reading through the telephone directory in the hope of discovering the address of the number on the notice. He was halfway through the Bakers when Mrs. Brogan discovered him.

"What are you doing?"

Robin looked at her helplessly and could think of no reply. "Come on down and stop worrying about that dog," Mrs. Brogan told him. "I know how you feel because I feel the same way myself, but sitting up here won't hurry the week along."

"Sun Dance asked me to help him burgle the police station," Robin told her. "I wish I could!"

"I've had a much better idea than that," said his mother. "Listen! If Friday is claimed, and I'm beginning to think he won't be, but if he is, I'm going to offer to buy him. What about that for a fallback plan?"

"Well, it's much better than Sun Dance's," said Robin gratefully.

"That's right!" agreed Mrs. Brogan. "Honesty is the best policy! And it's not that long till the weekend and we don't even think that anyone is looking for him, so you cheer up! Come downstairs and see what Mrs. Robinson's just brought round!"

Robin went downstairs with his mother's words ringing in his head. "Honesty is the best policy! . . . We don't even think anyone is looking for him!" The notice from the village shop was torn into fragments and buried at the bottom of the trash can, but he could not get rid of the telephone number so easily. He had tried to forget it but it would not go away. The honest thing to do would be to call that number and give Friday up.

Exclamations of admiration were coming from the kitchen. Mrs. Robinson, in an attempt to soothe her conscience, had baked an enormous chocolate cake and roasted a large turkey so that Mrs. Brogan would not have to worry about food. Old Blanket and the twins were in the kitchen, admiring them with hungry pride.

"You won't start eating them before we get here, will you?" asked Perry anxiously.

"I shouldn't think so," replied Mrs. Brogan.

On the Brogan front lawn Beany and Sun Dance were trying out their sleeping bags.

"We brought them now to save time tomorrow," Beany explained to Mrs. Brogan when she came out to inspect them.

"Do tramps have sleeping bags?" asked Sun Dance.

"I think some of them do," Mrs. Brogan replied.

"Do they eat turkey and chocolate cake?"

"If they can get it."

Sun Dance sighed with relief. Since the unhappy shopping trip he had lived largely on tomatoes, mostly out of sympathy with the tramps, but also in order to prove to Perry that such a diet was possible.

"Sun Dance," said Mrs. Brogan cautiously, "you'll have to stop worrying about those tramps, you know."

"Why?" asked Sun Dance. "They're still there, aren't they?"

"Some of them like being tramps."

"I'd hate it," said Sun Dance.

"It's very difficult to help them."

"It isn't," argued Sun Dance. "It's easy. I gave them tomatoes."

Mrs. Brogan gave up and went back indoors and Sun Dance and Beany continued to arrange their possessions.

They made a very good camp, especially when Beany had unpacked the two large suitcases of toys she had brought and Sun Dance had installed Chop Bone Man in Perry's sleeping bag.

"It looks like we've been here forever," said Beany proudly and Sun Dance agreed. They were trying to force Old Blanket into Ant's bag when a car pulled up in the road outside.

"Good Lord!" said the man who climbed out. "I telephoned a few days ago and the woman told me she had one quiet boy! Do you live here?"

"We're going to," said Beany proudly. "We're staying here, all of us."

"All of you?"

"Us and the twins but not Mum and Dad," explained Beany. "They're leaving us to do what we like! Midnight feasts and Murder in the Dark! But we've brought our own sleeping bags because Mrs. Brogan hates putting on clean sheets every day!"

"Do I remind you of a tramp?" inquired Sun Dance, but the people were not interested in replying. They muttered to each other and then climbed back into their car and drove away. Mrs. Brogan came running out of the house as they left.

"Who were those people?" she asked.

"No one nice," Beany told her.

"What did they say to you?"

"They asked if we lived here and said you said you had one quiet boy. They said they telephoned you."

"Good grief!" moaned Mrs. Brogan. "More customers gone!"

"Only horrible ones," said Beany cheerfully.

"It doesn't matter how horrible they are if they pay!" said Mrs. Brogan. "This is the worst summer I've had for years! It would make a nice change if you people could try charming my clients instead of chasing them off!"

Mrs. Robinson, arriving to collect her children, heard the end of this speech and she repeated it very forcefully to Beany and the twins that evening.

"Mrs. Brogan has a living to make and she works very hard and it isn't easy," she told them. "I want you three to promise you will behave yourselves tomorrow. She isn't expecting people to stay but if any should turn up you must be polite and quiet and do anything you can to help. If I hear that anyone has gone away because of anything any of you has done you will be in serious trouble!"

They nodded solemnly.

"And do what you can to help Robin," she added. "He worries too much!"

"All right," they agreed.

"And one last thing," she wound up. "That awful old heap of rubbish you've been carting around . . . those bones . . ."

"Do you mean Chop Bone Man?" asked Perry, hardly able to believe his ears.

"Either bury it or put it in the trash can," ordered his mother. "I don't want to see it again and I'm sure Mrs. Brogan doesn't, either! All right then, bath time, Beany! Sun Dance must be out by now. Up you come!"

The twins looked at each other when she had gone.

"We can't get rid of Chop Bone Man," said Ant. "It would hurt his feelings. And it would be a waste of Josephine's head."

"I don't see what we can do about Robin, either,"

added Perry. "Not about his dog anyway."

"He worries about other things as well as Friday," said Ant. "Things like them not having enough money and the bed and breakfasters not coming."

"I know," said Perry.

"Pity Beany and Sun Dance scared those two away."

"Yes."

"I wish we hadn't hung up Chop Bone Man."

"So do I now," said Perry. "Shut up a minute, Ant! I'm thinking!"

"What about?"

"Shut up!"

He closed his eyes and buried his head under a sofa cushion. Ant sat impatiently waiting for her brother to get his thoughts in order.

"Hurry up!"

Perry sat up and opened his eyes. "She ought to advertise," he announced.

"I thought you were thinking of something useful," said Ant, disappointed.

"I was. That's it."

"It's just what Dad always says."

"Well then," said Perry impatiently. "That proves I'm right! She should advertise and then people would come. But she doesn't."

"I wonder why not."

"It's probably too expensive for her."

"Yes," agreed Ant.

Perry looked at his sister to see if she was being extra slow on purpose but she merely looked puzzled and slightly bored.

"*We* could advertise, though!" he said. "We've got our birthday money! We could put it in the paper!"

"We don't know how! And anyway, what if it doesn't work?" protested Ant.

"At least we'll have tried. And if it doesn't it won't have cost Robin's mum anything and if it does it will make up for Chop Bone Man."

Ant still looked very unconvinced but Perry bounded away to the room he shared with Sun Dance and returned a minute later with a copy of the local paper from the previous week.

"There!" he said triumphantly, turning to the advertisements at the back. "I knew I'd seen it! There's a form you fill in. Seventeen pence a word!"

"Pence?" asked Ant, becoming more hopeful. "I thought it would be pounds."

"Pence it says," said Perry, pointing, "and there's stacks of other advertisements. We only need copy the sort of thing they put."

"What else do we have to do?"

"Nothing," said Perry. "There's nothing to it! Write down what you want to put. Work out the money, fill in the form, and one of us can leave it at the newspaper office tonight. It's only next door to the post office. We can be there and back in ten minutes. 'Three working days before the date of the next edition to guarantee publication' it says. That means this Friday if we're lucky and next Friday if we're not. Even that wouldn't be too late. There's plenty of summer left."

"What'll we put?" asked Ant, beginning to be enthusiastic.

"'Bed and Breakfasters Wanted,'" said Perry.

"What else? We ought to put something that'll make them really want to come. Something like 'Good Food.'"

"Just good food isn't enough," objected Perry. "We want something really exciting! Ghosts! 'Good Food and Ghosts at Sea View!'"

"'Good Food and Ghosts at Porridge Hall' sounds better," said Ant. "I think Porridge Hall is a lovely name, but there aren't any ghosts."

"We could easily arrange a few ghosts if we tried," said Perry impatiently.

Ant was studying the other bed-and-breakfast advertisements in the paper.

"They say things like 'Hot and Cold and Television,'" she said.

"Hot and Cold what?"

"Water, of course," said Perry. "It's a pity Mrs. Brogan hasn't got televisions in her rooms."

"She's got a lovely garden, though," said Ant, "and she lets the bed and breakfasters in it."

"Well then, we'll put: 'Hot and Cold Water. No television. Garden instead.'"

"'Well-trained dogs and children welcome,'" suggested Ant.

"That sounds like the children have to be well trained as well as the dogs."

"'Well-trained dogs and ordinary children'?"

"That's better. And then the telephone number. And they always seem to say something like 'Friendly Staff,' or 'Warm Welcome,' or 'Family Owners.'"

"Mrs. Brogan is nice but she's not always friendly.

She can be very fierce."

"Well, we'll put 'quite friendly' then. She is that."

> Bed and Breakfasters Wanted.
> Good Food (and Ghosts) at Porridge Hall.
> Hot and Cold Water. No television. Garden instead.
> Well-trained dogs and ordinary children welcome.
> Telephone 555-5703. Owner quite friendly.

"Thirty words," said Ant, writing carefully and counting up. How much is that?"

"Seventeen thirties?" Perry shouted upstairs to Sun Dance, and a moment later the reply came.

"Five hundred and ten."

"Five pounds and ten pence," said Perry, "and another one pound fifty to put lines round it. It looks much posher with lines round it, I think."

"Six pounds and sixty pence, then," said Ant. "Three pounds thirty each. That's not bad!"

Perry agreed and six pound coins and three twenty pences were put into an envelope with the form. Ant went up for her bath and Perry slipped out of the house and sprinted down the road to the newspaper office. He pushed the envelope through the door and returned feeling that Mrs. Brogan's fortune was as good as made.

"Done it," he whispered to Ant.

"Done what?" asked Mrs. Robinson, overhearing.

"Nothing much," replied Perry and Ant together.

Mrs. Robinson looked at the twins suspiciously but her mind was too full of plans and instructions for the next day to wonder about the matter for long.

"You won't forget what I told you about tomorrow?" she asked.

"'Course not."

"Quiet, helpful, and polite?"

"We know."

"And . . . ?"

"What?"

"Those awful bones," prompted Mrs. Robinson.

"Oh Mum!" protested Perry and Ant together.

"It's no good Oh Mumming me!" replied Mrs. Robinson. "I was ashamed of you hanging them up under Mrs. Brogan's sign! And, anyway, they're not clean."

"What if we wash them?" suggested Perry.

"No," said Mrs. Robinson.

"We could give him to Robin, I suppose," said Ant.

"Oh no you couldn't," replied her mother so firmly that they gave up arguing. They waited until the next morning and then, when their parents (issuing orders to the last) had finally departed, they broke the news to Robin and Sun Dance.

"What exactly doesn't she like about him?" asked Robin.

"She doesn't think he looks nice," explained Ant.

Everyone looked thoughtfully at Chop Bone Man, who had been hauled out for the occasion.

"He doesn't look nice," agreed Robin, "but he's not meant to."

"Perhaps he'd look better dressed," suggested Beany.

"Waste of his bones," said Robin.

"Depends what we dress him in," said Perry, suddenly

inspired. "If we made him a suit of armor Mum would never want him thrown away! We could stand him by the front door to surprise people!"

Only Robin seemed to doubt their ability to make a suit of armor, and he had reckoned without the ingenuity of his neighbors. By lunchtime Chop Bone Man wore a vest of hammered flat tin cans threaded together with string through nail-punched holes. An old cookie jar made a splendid helmet, and more tin cans, with the bottoms cut out as well as the tops, made sleeves that bent at the elbows. Old Blanket obligingly ate two cans of dog food for his lunch and thus provided gauntlets.

"If I had a suit of armor like that I could fight Dan easy," remarked Sun Dance.

At one o'clock they broke off to make devastating inroads on the turkey and chocolate cake.

"What shall we do about his legs?" asked Ant. "We've run out of cans."

"Rolled-up paper?" suggested Mrs. Brogan. "Then I wouldn't have to worry about you cutting yourselves."

"Paper would spoil it," said Ant. "We won't cut ourselves! We haven't done all morning."

"You've been lucky, then," said Mrs. Brogan. "Doubly lucky; because if I'd known you were chopping open tin cans I'd have stopped you."

"We didn't let Beany chop and Sun Dance didn't want to."

"I hate Chop Bone Man," said Sun Dance suddenly. "Do you know what I think of when I look at him?"

"What?" asked Robin.

"Blood," said Sun Dance. "Blood, blood, blood!"

"That settles it," said Mrs. Brogan. "I'd rather you found something else to do this afternoon. I'm not having Sun Dance frightened!"

They spent a happy hour or so playing soccer, taking it in turns to be in goal and counting up the scores. Dan, passing the garden, looked over the wall rather wistfully.

"Come and play," said Ant. "Then we could be three a side!"

For a moment it seemed that Dan was tempted, but then he remembered that he was talking to the enemy.

"I don't play with girls," he said. "Or nutters or thieves!"

"What did he mean?" demanded Sun Dance furiously.

"Take no notice," said Robin uneasily, and they tried to, but it had spoiled the afternoon. First Beany wandered off and then Robin took Sun Dance inside to inspect the twenty cans of dog food and to admire Friday's new collar and leash. Only the twins were left outside.

"It's a pity we're not to do Chop Bone Man's suit of armor," said Ant. "Because I've thought of something brilliant for his legs!"

"She only said she'd rather we didn't," pointed out Perry. "She didn't say we couldn't."

"Come on then!" said Ant.

There was the remains of an ancient greenhouse at the bottom of the Robinsons' garden, which Mr. Robinson had not yet found time to demolish. It had once been heated by a small iron stove, and the stovepipe, exactly the right size for legs of a suit of armor and jointed at convenient intervals, poked out of the roof. Ant took Perry down to the greenhouse and silently pointed.

"Perfect!" said Perry.

The pipe was fastened by bolts where it came out through the roof, and since they could not loosen it from below, Perry and Ant, forgetting Sun Dance's warning and what small amount of common sense they possessed, climbed up to shake it free. A moment later they crashed through the roof together, bringing with them an avalanche of broken glass and landing on the stove.

"Crikey!" said Ant as she picked herself up. "Look at your legs!"

"Look at yours!" said Perry. "I bet you need more stitches!"

It seemed more than likely. Ant was looking very pale, and sticky rivulets of blood were running down their bare legs and beginning to soak into their socks. By the time they had extracted themselves and collected the stovepipe they were in a state of gore spectacular even by Robinson standards.

"It won't be much fun telling Mrs. Brogan," said Perry.

"I do feel queer," said Ant. "I wonder how Sun Dance knew."

"Knew what?"

"Blood, blood, blood!" said Ant, and fainted.

five
• • • • •

"Guests tonight!" said Mrs. Brogan, putting down the telephone receiver and smiling very cheerfully at Robin, Beany, and Sun Dance, who were with her in the kitchen.

"How many?" asked Robin.

"Only two, but they said they'd like to stay two nights at least, and perhaps more. They sounded nice, young for a change and interested in the coast. They asked about fossils and the birds on the cliffs. We must make them welcome. They don't sound the usual sort at all!"

"What are the usual sort?" asked Sun Dance.

"Oh," said Mrs. Brogan, "middle-aged, fussy, penny-pinching, don't like children . . ."

"Or even worse, do like children," put in Robin, "and bring their own, who poke about my bedroom and touch my things."

"Smoke in their rooms, which I loathe . . ." continued Mrs. Brogan.

"Pinch the towels!" interrupted Robin.

"Pinch the towels," agreed Mrs. Brogan. "Back their cars into the roses, block up the drains with their falling-out hair, leave paper handkerchiefs under the pillows . . ."

"Allergic to dairy products and wheat," said Robin, remembering a pair who had arrived that spring.

"Allergic to dairy products and wheat, sit on the beach with next to nothing on and then complain about the cold wind, steal the toilet paper rolls, pay with bad checks, put spare slices of toast in their handbags at breakfast time, break things and hide them, pick my flowers . . ."

"Why don't you just tell them not to?" asked Beany.

"Not that easy," said Mrs. Brogan. "Oh well! It will be nice to have intelligent people to stay for once!"

"Where will they sleep?" asked Beany. "I could help you get it ready."

"Thanks, but the big room at the front is ready. You could put in some flowers if you like . . . PERRY!!!"

Everyone turned to stare at Perry, who stood grinning sheepishly in the kitchen doorway. He had guessed that Mrs. Brogan would not be pleased to see him and he was right.

"I'm all right," said Perry, trying to appear unaware of the fact that he was covered with blood, "but Ant's fainted . . . only a bit, though," he added in an attempt to make the best of a bad situation.

Even as he spoke, Mrs. Brogan, white with horror, was pushing past him.

"Where is she?"

"By the greenhouse. We fell through the roof. Not your greenhouse," he added, seeing the direction in which she was heading and trundling after her, "ours. Yours is quite all right!"

But Mrs. Brogan, racing through the gardens in search of her neighbors' child, was far too frightened to think about the state of her greenhouse. She was imagining Ant, broken-necked or bleeding to death, and she was saying over and over again as she ran, "Whatever will I say to your mother? Whatever will I say to your mother?"

"She won't mind," said Ant, struggling to her feet on the Robinsons' lawn. "She's used to us."

Then Mrs. Brogan stopped being frightened and started being furious. She was angrier than Robin had ever seen her before. Her eyes glittered with rage and she snapped questions at the twins as if she hated them. She heard how they had come to fall through the greenhouse roof, and Sun Dance waited hopefully for her to pronounce suitable hangings or drownings or floggings, but he waited in vain. She bathed their cuts and examined their bruises and marched them out to the car.

"Where are we going?" quavered Perry, awed by her anger.

"Stitches and tetanus injections," she answered briefly.

"Jabs?" they asked together in horror.

"We've had them," protested Ant. "I'm sure we have."

"I'm taking no chances," said Mrs. Brogan. "You'll probably need some stitches too."

"They don't mind the stitches," Beany explained. "It's the jabs they hate."

"Good," said Mrs. Brogan. "They deserve far worse than that! When I saw Perry standing in that door my heart nearly stopped! They deserve a thorough beating!"

It was such a relief to hear her prescribing punishments in her usual voice instead of the silent white-faced raging of the last few minutes that everyone smiled.

"You may laugh!" she said, "but it's no laughing matter. I've guests due tonight and goodness knows when we'll get back! Robin, I'm terribly sorry but I'll have to leave you in charge. I'd take Sun Dance and Beany with me but we might be there half the night. Don't let them onto the road or the beach and don't do anything stupid. Please! And try and make those people welcome if they turn up."

"We will. Don't worry!"

"I have to go then. I'll call if I can call, but don't worry if I don't. Perhaps we won't be long . . ."

She hovered, worried and uncertain, wondering if she dared leave them.

"Go," said Robin, "and then you'll be back quicker. We'll be all right."

"I have to," she said. "I really have to. Those cuts are such a mess. Deep and dirty . . ."

"We're awfully sorry," said Ant miserably.

"Blood, blood, blood," said Sun Dance. "Just like I said!"

"Yes, just like you said," agreed Mrs. Brogan. "You will be sensible, Sun Dance, won't you?"

"I always am," said Sun Dance.

For a little while after the car had driven away they sat by the steps and talked.

"Your poor mum," said Beany.

"What about poor Perry and Ant?" asked Sun Dance.

"Serve them right," said Beany ruthlessly, and Robin wholeheartedly agreed. He knew perfectly well that the Robinson children had been invited for the express purpose of taking his mind off his troubles and he felt at least partly responsible.

"What shall we do if those bed and breakfasters come?" asked Beany.

"Try and keep them," replied Robin. "I'm not going to let them go if I can help it."

"Neither will I," promised Beany, "and neither will Sun Dance, will you, Sun Dance?"

"Blood, blood, blood!" said Sun Dance with satisfaction.

"Well, there's no need to sound so pleased!" said Robin.

Presently Sun Dance said he thought he would go and inspect the remains of the greenhouse and Robin went with him to make sure no more accidents took place. Beany was left alone, and having nothing better to do she went and found a spade and was soon engaged in digging a pond by the front door to cheer up Mrs. Brogan when she came back. She was so engrossed that she did not notice the two people walking down the path until they stood in front of her.

"Hello!" said the woman, looking down on her.

"Hello," said Beany, glancing briefly up from her hole.

"Is it all right if we come past?" asked the woman. "We wanted to see your mother. We were hoping to stay for a few days."

"Oh!" exclaimed Beany. "Are you the bed and breakfasters who telephoned this morning? Fossils and birds? More intelligent than usual?"

"I think that must be us," agreed the man.

"Mrs. Brogan said she thought you were quite young," explained Beany. "That's why I didn't guess it was you."

"We are quite young," said the man.

"Oh," said Beany. "I thought you looked nearly as old as my mum."

It was obvious that the bed and breakfasters were very tempted to ask how old Beany's mum was but they did not need to.

"She's thirty-five," Beany told them. "She's going to shoot herself when she's forty, she says. What do you want to see her for?"

"Doesn't she live here?"

"Oh no," said Beany.

"Then who's in charge?"

Beany explained that Robin was in charge, with her to help, and that she was digging a pond.

"For whom?" asked the man. "Robin?"

"For fish," said Beany patiently. "Only this patch of ground seems to be full of rocks. If you come inside I'll show you your room. It's all got ready."

"Thank you," they said and followed her inside and upstairs.

"Its very nice," she told them as she led them in, determined that these bed and breakfasters, at least, should not escape. "I picked some flowers but I could get a different sort if you don't like them. And there's tea and coffee and a kettle and a little package of free chocolate cookies."

"Very nice," said the woman.

"Clean sheets," continued Beany, admiring herself in the full-length mirror. "Clean sheets, not just smoothed down and put back on! And there's a bathroom next door with free soap and bubblebath, only don't pinch the towels, will you?"

She gazed at them worriedly and they hurriedly agreed not to pinch the towels.

"Or use all the hot water or block up the drain with your falling-out hair?" she continued anxiously.

"Of course not," said the woman, while the man stared out of the window and shook. "You haven't asked our names yet, have you? We're Mr. and Mrs. Moore. Ann and John. And now I really think we ought to see your mother."

"I'm Beany," said Beany, "but you can't see my mother. She's not here. She went ages ago."

"What about Robin, then? We were wondering if we could get an evening meal here."

"Wondering what?" asked Beany.

"If we could have anything to eat."

"'Course you can!" said Beany, who would have agreed to anything rather than lose her captives. "I didn't know you were hungry! I'll go and tell Robin now."

"I wonder who on earth Robin is," said Ann Moore as Beany ran downstairs, and she wondered still more when Beany returned to say they could have supper if turkey would do and that Sun Dance said they ought to have soup and that both Robin and Sun Dance agreed that they would have to pay extra.

"Is he crying?" she mouthed in a silent whisper to Mrs. Moore, gazing worriedly at Mr. Moore, who was holding his head in his hands and appeared to be sobbing out of the window.

"Oh no," said Mrs. Moore. "Take no notice!"

Beany nodded understandingly and pretended not to have seen that there were tears on Mr. Moore's cheeks.

"About supper," she continued. "We hope you'll like it. Robin is rather bothered but Sun Dance is helping him to get it ready. He's holding it down. Have you got plenty of money?"

"Yes, thank you," said Mrs. Moore. "Why do you ask?"

"Food is ten pounds extra," explained Beany. "But you can have as much to eat as you like and it's ready now. They've laid the table and they're hotting up the soup. Tomato."

Down in the kitchen, Robin was cutting bread and butter and worrying.

"Mum never does evening meals," he told Beany crossly. "She says it's more trouble than it's worth! I wish she'd hurry up and come back. I'm not waiting on them, you know!"

"Neither am I," agreed Sun Dance. "I'm a tramp, not a waiter!"

"I'll do it," said Beany serenely. "I don't mind. I went to a restaurant once and people did it to me and it's easy as pie. It's only carrying plates."

"Well, you'd better wash your hands first," ordered Robin, chopping away at the turkey while Sun Dance held it down.

"I have done," said Beany. "They're as clean as they'll come. I've been digging a pond to surprise your mum."

Robin groaned in horror.

"A pond would be lovely," said Sun Dance when Beany had returned to her guests. "The dogs could swim in it. Old Blanket's a brilliant swimmer. I bet he could teach Friday."

At that moment Friday seemed to Robin to be as unlikely a dream as Beany's pond. All the fates appeared to be against him that week and he became even more gloomy when Sun Dance peered around the kitchen door across to the dining room and reported that Beany was sitting at the table with the bed and breakfasters.

"Don't you want soup?" Mr. Moore asked Beany. He had recovered himself enough to eat, but he was still rather red about the eyes, Beany noticed.

"There was only one can," she replied with awful honesty. "Anyway, I'm saving room so I can eat more turkey. Robin's getting it ready now."

"We've been wondering," said Mrs. Moore. "Who is Sun Dance? Is he your dog?"

"Sun Dance a dog?" asked Beany, astonished. "He's my brother! He's older than me! He's helping Robin in the kitchen."

Mrs. Moore looked very relieved. She was pleased to hear that whatever was being held down in the kitchen in preparation for her supper was being held down by human hands, but she could not resist one more question.

"Robin is the chef?"

"The what?" asked Beany.

"Does the cooking?"

"Oh yes," said Beany.

"Is he older than Sun Dance, then?"

"Oh yes," said Beany. "Much older. And brainier. Would you like any more soup? There's a bit more in the saucepan but I didn't put it in in case it slopped over the sides of the plates."

"No more soup, thank you," said Mrs. Moore. "It was very nice, though." And Mr. Moore, who still looked about to burst into tears at any moment, nodded in agreement.

"You can have your turkey, then," said Beany. "Do you want it cold on a plate or in sandwiches?"

Mr. and Mrs. Moore, who despite their fears about Robin, had been hungrily hoping for it roasted and hot and with vegetables, looked extremely surprised.

"Cold on a plate," replied Mrs. Moore, pulling herself together and glaring at her weeping husband. "With salad would be nice. Who is Robin?"

"He lives here," explained Beany. "Salad, well, I don't know. There might be some tomatoes if Sun Dance hasn't eaten them."

"Is he fond of tomatoes?" asked Mr. Moore.

"Yes, but that's not why he eats them," said Beany. "He eats them because of the tramps. If you like lettuce I could pull one up out of the garden if you don't mind waiting while we wash it."

The Moores replied that they didn't mind waiting at all and through the window they watched Beany run across the lawn to the greenhouse and return a moment later with a lettuce in each hand.

"I'm beginning to think she runs this place single-handed," remarked Mrs. Moore. "I do wish you would try and get a grip on yourself a bit. She thinks you're crying!"

"I am," said Mr. Moore. "And of course she doesn't do it single-handed. Someone hotted up the soup!"

In a shorter time than they would have believed possible the lettuce was on their plates, together with turkey, tomatoes, and a great deal of bread and butter.

"Robin says," said Beany, tucking in with gusto, "if you want salad dressing could you pay now and Sun Dance will go and buy some. We've run out."

Mr. Moore suddenly choked, and Mrs. Moore, after thumping him on the back several times, replied that they would manage very well as they were.

"Tell us about yourself," she suggested. "What did you say your name was and who did I speak to on the phone? Are Robin and Sun Dance having any supper? Who cooked this lovely turkey?"

"My mum did before she went away," replied Beany, answering the easiest question first. "Sun Dance said he just wanted chocolate cake for supper and Robin isn't hungry because he's worrying too much."

"Not about us, I hope?"

"Oh no," said Beany reassuringly. "About his dog. He's been worrying about it all week. They said you could have chocolate cake next if you like, or else Sun Dance's special pudding that he said he would make for you."

The Moores unhesitatingly chose Sun Dance's special pudding and when it arrived it looked so much like slices of bread and jam with milk poured over it and ice cream on top that Mrs. Moore, carefully avoiding her husband's eyes, asked how it was made.

"It's slices of bread and jam with milk poured over it and ice cream on top," Beany told her. "It's lovely, isn't it? In winter we have it with hot milk and no ice cream."

Her guests agreed that it was delicious, and spooned in soggy bread and jam with every appearance of enjoyment.

"When Robin saw it he said you'd never eat it," remarked Beany. "He's gone into the garden because he's ashamed. He said we shouldn't charge you because the turkey was left over from dinner and anyway he got it free and the lettuce was out of the garden and the soup was an ancient old can out of the back of the cupboard, but Sun Dance says we still should. Unless you're tramps."

"We're not tramps," said Mrs. Moore.

"Good," said Beany, and she gazed hopefully at Mr. Moore, but he showed no signs of getting out his wallet.

"Don't you think you would like to pay now before you finish," she suggested gently. "In case you forget?"

The hospital had been very busy and Mrs. Brogan had had to wait a long time before Perry and Ant were seen. They were both given tetanus injections and Ant had three blue thread stitches in her leg, which cheered her immensely. It was after eight o'clock before they reached home again, and they arrived just in time to see Beany accepting her ten-pound note from Mrs. Moore.

"Are you sure you can afford it?" Beany asked anxiously, and she regarded the silently weeping Mr. Moore with great concern.

"Quite sure," said Mrs. Moore. "Don't you worry about him, either," she added, frowning at her husband. "You're perfectly all right, aren't you, John?"

Mr. Moore nodded but made no reply. Tears ran down his cheeks and every now and then he bent over and slapped his knees. He had been in this state ever since Sun Dance had arrived from the kitchen and begun to swap recipes with his wife.

"Look what we've got!" said Beany as Mrs. Brogan rushed into the room. "Bed and breakfasters! We've fed them and everything! And told them about the towels and the drains and they've paid for their supper already! And they'd have paid for their bed as well but I thought it would be fairer if I went in and got it when they woke up. Or you did," she added as an afterthought, suddenly remembering she was no longer in charge.

"BEANY!" exclaimed Mrs. Brogan, and then for some time it was not perfectly clear to Beany whether she was supposed to have behaved very very well or very very badly. Sun Dance would have been in no doubt that they had been nothing less than heroes if it had not been for Robin, whose courage had failed him at the sight of Sun Dance's pudding. He seemed to think they had disgraced the Brogan good name forever. Beany was quite bewildered until Mr. and Mrs. Moore came to the rescue.

Never, they told Mrs. Brogan, had they had such an entertaining hostess as Beany, or enjoyed a pudding so much as Sun Dance's, or heard of such an honest cook as Robin. Where was the honest cook, they asked, and incidentally, how old was he? Mrs. Brogan, still very cross but cooling off already, told them that he was nearly eleven years old, plenty old enough to have more sense, and she added that she had no idea where he was. There followed a short investigation during which it was discovered that the honest cook had prudently gone to bed.

"And that's where the rest of you are going," she told them. "Out of sight and out of mind!"

Beany was chased upstairs immediately and Perry and Ant, still too subdued to argue very much, soon followed.

"What about Murder in the Dark and our midnight feast?" Sun Dance asked.

Mrs. Brogan replied that all the murder in the dark carried out that night would be the result of her discovering midnight feasters, but as usual, her bark was far worse than her bite. She went into the kitchen to prepare sandwiches and milk for the injured and disgraced while Sun Dance lingered talking to Mr. Moore.

"Why were you crying?" asked Sun Dance.

"Don't you ever laugh so much you cry?" asked Mr. Moore.

"Laugh so much I cry?" repeated Sun Dance.

"Yes."

"No, I don't," said Sun Dance. "No one does."

"I do," said Mr. Moore.

"I cry," said Sun Dance, "and I laugh. But not together. I don't laugh much, though. Do you ever cry so much you laugh?"

"No," said Mr. Moore. "Do you?"

"No," said Sun Dance, and there was a long pause in the conversation.

"I wish I'd met Robin," said Mr. Moore.

"He'll be glad you didn't," said Sun Dance. "He hates people crying. He hates fuss. He's fed up."

"What about?"

"His dog."

"Oh, yes," said Mr. Moore, remembering. "Beany mentioned a dog."

"They've taken him away and we can't get him back," explained Sun Dance. "He's called Friday."

"That's a good name."

"Short for Dog Friday. Those ancient laws don't work at all. Now Robin worries about him all the time like I worry about my tramps."

"I understand," said Mr. Moore. "So Robin's lost his dog, has he? I lost a dog when I was a boy."

"Did you get it back?"

"No," said Mr. Moore. "What were you telling me about those tramps?"

"Where do you think they get their food from?" asked Sun Dance. "Sometimes I can't work out what to do about everything."

"What sort of everything?"

"Robin's dog and Dan's nose and ancient laws if nobody takes any notice of them and what to do about tramps with no food." As Sun Dance spoke he became more excited, pacing between the door and the window and twisting the front of his T-shirt into a damp and grubby knot.

"Nobody knows all the answers," said Mr. Moore, speaking quietly so that Sun Dance would have to stand still and listen. "There's always more questions than there are answers, and the questions are just as important. Even if you don't know what to do it's still a good thing to ask the questions."

Sun Dance did not think that reply much help at all but he recognized that Mr. Moore was trying to comfort him, and he was grateful.

"I'll make you another pudding tomorrow, if you like," he offered, and he went to bed quite happily, thinking of variations. He thought he might use honey instead of jam, and orange juice instead of milk, and he fell asleep in the middle of wondering what to use instead of ice cream.

Mr. Moore mentioned that he'd been talking to Sun Dance when he said good-night to Mrs. Brogan.

"Poor old Sun Dance," she said. "Nothing leaves that child."

Mrs. Moore looked puzzled but her husband understood immediately. He had once known someone a little like Sun Dance before, someone whose thoughts and experiences and emotions did not drift in and out of their minds, like most people's do, but stayed there, piled in heaps and making a tremendous muddle. Sun Dance tried to make sense of his heap of muddled thoughts. He climbed on top and called to the world about ancient laws and burglars and tramps and tomatoes, and of course no one understood. It did not make sense to anyone, least of all Sun Dance.

"Poor old Sun Dance," agreed Mr. Moore.

* * *

Robin woke up on Thursday morning and it was seven o'clock. That meant if nothing went wrong in thirty-five hours' time, Friday would have served his seven day sentence and should be free to return to Robin. One hundred and thirty-three hours gone, calculated Robin, and thirty-five more to go. He was getting very good at the twenty-four times table. He checked in his head to see if he could still remember the telephone number on the notice and guiltily found that he could.

Across the hall, from the family room, came cheering, distracting noises. It was the sound of the Robinson children getting up and Robin had been hearing it on and off all night long because the family room contained two single beds and a set of bunk beds, and everyone wanted to sleep in the top bunk. There had been no quarreling about this matter because Ant had thoughtfully brought with her their parents' alarm clock. They set it to go off at two-hour intervals all through the night and every time it rang all four of them got up and swapped beds. Luckily the Moores were sleeping on the other side of the house but Mrs. Brogan heard the one o'clock change and got up to investigate.

"What is it?" Robin had asked when she looked in on him, on her way back to bed.

"It's the sound of democracy at work," she said. "Go to sleep!"

Shortly after seven o'clock democracy broke down. Sun Dance, who was occupying the top bunk, refused to leave his high position, claiming that it was daytime now and nighttime agreements no longer held. When Robin came in to say good morning he found Sun Dance defending himself bravely while Beany hurled the contents of her suitcase at him and Perry and Ant tried to unseat him by pushing up the mattress from underneath.

"Help, Robin!" he shouted, and Robin leaped up beside him and then doubled up with pain, clutching his knee.

"What on earth have you got in your sleeping bag?" he demanded, and was not very surprised when Sun Dance unzipped it to show Chop Bone Man, dressed half in a suit of armor and half in a pair of Beany's old jeans.

"Did you sleep with Chop Bone Man?" he asked.

"Partly," said Sun Dance vaguely.

Robin leaned over the side of the bunk to look down on the twins.

"Are you better this morning?" he asked.

"'Course," said Perry. "We were better last night only we didn't like to say so."

"My stitches are pulling a bit but that's all," remarked Ant.

"Stitches always do at first," said Perry.

"I know," said Ant and bent over to try and lick them. Robin could not help feeling they were remarkably cheerful considering the disgrace they had been in the previous night. Neither of them showed the slightest signs of remorse. Even when Robin hinted that his mother had not been exactly delighted with their behavior they merely grinned at each other.

"Don't worry," said Perry. "We're making it up to her!"

"How?" asked Robin, alarmed, but they refused to say.

"You'll see," said Perry, and renewed the assault on the top bunk. A moment later Mrs. Brogan stuck her head around the door.

"It sounds like the kitchen ceiling is coming down," she told them. "Either get up or go back to bed, but do it quietly!"

"All right," said Sun Dance, sliding in beside Chop Bone Man. "Me and Robin won anyway!"

"You and Robin and Chop Bone Man!" said Perry. "What a team!"

"We are a team," said Sun Dance, when Robin had gone to get dressed. "I help Robin and Robin helps me. It's a pity his name is Robin instead of Butch Cassidy."

"Don't suppose Robin thinks it is," said Ant, "and I haven't noticed you helping him much! It's usually the other way round!"

"It isn't!" said Sun Dance indignantly. "I went to the police station to try and get Friday! I helped him look after those bed and breakfasters last night! What about that fantastic pudding I made!"

"S'pose you did," agreed Ant amiably. "Did they really like it?"

"They loved it," said Sun Dance proudly. "You ask them!"

As it turned out, nobody had a chance to ask the Moores anything that morning. Mrs. Brogan, feeling that she really could not afford to lose any more bed and breakfasters, cunningly contrived that her two sets of guests would not meet. It was not until late afternoon, when the telephone rang, that Mr. Moore met his honest cook for the first time. He had just come through the front door when Robin, leaping down all five steps of the last flight of stairs, landed fair and square in the middle of his chest.

"I'm terribly sorry," said Robin. "I thought it might be the police about Friday."

"No harm done," said Mr. Moore cheerfully, and he listened, looking almost as concerned as Robin, while Mrs. Brogan answered the phone. It was not the police, however, it was only Mrs. Robinson, checking for the third time during her brief escape that her children were still surviving.

"Did I hurt you?" asked Robin, when his mother had returned to the kitchen.

"Not at all," said Mr. Moore. "And I can understand you worrying. Sun Dance told us last night about you losing your dog. I lost a dog myself once when I was a boy!"

"Sun Dance told us you did," replied Robin, "and he told us you never got him back."

"No," said Mr. Moore. "Well, it was all a long time ago, a very long time ago, Beany might say! And it wasn't even my dog, it belonged to my grandparents. I lived with them, you see. But I've always regretted losing that dog. I didn't go about looking for him properly."

"What do you mean?" asked Robin, and a miserable cold feeling began to grow in his heart.

"Oh, I cycled miles, you know, day after day, searching and calling. Asking people. Forgot completely about doing the obvious thing, contacting the police, and no one thought to remind me. My grandparents were very old, and there wasn't really anyone . . ." He stopped, catching sight of Robin's stricken face.

"I shouldn't be talking to you like this! You're doing

it right anyway! I just thought I'd say, you know, that I know how you feel."

"Perhaps someone nice found your dog and he went to a good home."

"Yes," agreed Mr. Moore. "Perhaps he did. Anyway he must have gone years ago. Funny, but I've never stopped looking for him!"

Robin scarcely knew what he replied, or how he got away from Mr. Moore, but as soon as he could he was at the telephone, dialing the number on the notice. He prayed that nobody would answer and nobody did.

six
• • • •

Late on Thursday afternoon Mr. and Mrs. Robinson arrived home with a car piled high with shopping and presents.

"It's more than ten years since we spent a day without the children," remarked Mrs. Robinson, and her husband, staggering under heaps of boxes and shopping bags, said it would be more than ten years before they could afford to do it again. They had brought something for everyone, including Old Blanket and Friday.

"You'd better not hand that over yet," commented Mr. Robinson when he noticed the new blanket they'd bought for Friday, and Mrs. Robinson agreed and put it out of sight.

"It looks like Christmas," said Robin as he unpacked a new, unpunctured football to replace the one that had floated away.

"Travelers should always buy presents for the stay-at-homes," replied Mr. Robinson.

Beany pointed out that they had only been away one

night but her mother said it felt more like six weeks and Mrs. Brogan privately agreed. So far nothing had been said about the twins and the greenhouse roof. Mrs. Brogan, when asked if her guests had been good, had merely smiled and said they had been no worse than usual.

"What did you buy for Chop Bone Man?" asked Sun Dance when everything had been unwrapped and inspected.

"I THOUGHT I TOLD YOU TO GET RID OF THAT THING!" exclaimed his mother.

"You said you didn't want to see him again so we made him a suit of armor to cover him up!"

"Shut up, Sun Dance," muttered Ant.

Mrs. Robinson looked at Ant suspiciously.

"You made him what?" she asked Sun Dance.

"A suit of armor! But we didn't finish it because Ant and Perry fell through the greenhouse roof when they tried to get his trousers. You should see their legs! They had to go to the hospital!"

"Thank you, Sun Dance!" said Mrs. Brogan crossly. "I hoped to break that piece of news a little more tactfully!"

After that there was no peace at all. The twins were forced to take off their jeans and display their wounds and Mrs. Robinson inspected them furiously and unsympathetically.

"As if Mrs. Brogan hadn't enough to do without all the fuss and trouble you must have caused!" she exclaimed.

"Oh, it wasn't that bad," said Mrs. Brogan. "Beany held the fort most heroically. And they behaved very well at the hospital. They've had tetanus shots again just in case."

"They'd have had worse than that if I'd been about," said Mr. Robinson. "Of all the stupid, thoughtless, idiotic things to do! And if your mother told you to get rid of that bone thing you can do it now!"

"You haven't even seen his new suit of armor," protested Perry, but to no avail. He and Ant were marched out of the house and down to the end of their garden, where Mr. Robinson personally superintended the digging of Chop Bone Man's grave. Ant was excused the heaviest spadework because of her stitches, but was made to help with the filling in.

"Right," said Mr. Robinson when Chop Bone Man had been laid to rest and stamped down hard. "Bath! Bed! What on earth are you both sniveling about?"

"Poor Chop Bone Man," said Ant. "He must wonder what he's done!"

But if Mr. Robinson cared at all about Chop Bone Man's feelings he hid it very well. He laughed at Ant's tears and Perry's sniffs and callously forced the bereaved to clean the spade. Then he extracted a promise that they would not dig up the corpse in the morning and sent them to bed. Neither of them remembered that Thursday evening was the day the local paper was delivered. Exhausted by the combination of excitement and undertaking, they fell asleep.

It was Sun Dance who found the newspaper. It arrived when his mother was upstairs and his father was next door filling in Beany's pond. No one noticed when he took the paper upstairs to read in bed. Even if they had they would not have thought it unusual. It was always Sun Dance who grabbed the paper and searched through it for items on local burglaries and other bad but fascinating news.

That night Sun Dance clattered through the pages in his usual fashion. They contained very little interesting news that week, no burglaries, nothing about tramps or dogs or ancient laws. There was a pudding recipe that he read with scorn and a page of very unexciting letters. Sun Dance turned to the back and there wasn't any football news. In desperation he began to read the ads and long before he got to the one for Porridge Hall he found something that had a dramatic effect on him. It frightened him terribly. He hid the paper under his mattress but he was still scared. Later on, in the middle of the night, his whole family were awoken by Sun Dance shrieking and struggling in alarm and anger. In the morning he could not remember a thing about it.

On Friday morning Mr. and Mrs. Moore left, promising to return at the end of the summer and saying they would recommend Mrs. Brogan's hospitality to anyone.

"Not to mention your next-door neighbors' catering," added Mr. Moore. "I shan't forget Sun Dance's pudding for a long time! Or the turkey that had to be held down! And good luck to the honest cook!"

Robin grinned sheepishly.

"They've restored my faith in bed and breakfasters!" said Mrs. Brogan after they had driven away. A few moments later her faith was further encouraged when the mailman arrived with a large package. It contained eight towels, newly washed, a box of chocolates, and a letter of apology.

We could not believe, said the letter, *that we had packed eight towels by mistake! Goodness knows what you thought of us!*

"You thought they should be strangled!" Robin reminded her. "You said you'd do it yourself!"

"Of course I didn't!" said Mrs. Brogan.

"Cheerfully!" Robin told her. "That's what you said!"

"Oh, shut up!" said his mother. She was so pleased with her package that she went next door to tell the good news to Mrs. Robinson. While she was gone Robin forced himself to call the phone number on the notice. Once again there was no answer.

Robin let the telephone ring ten times and then put the receiver down. Twice now he had tried to contact them, and he thought that was more than they deserved.

That morning the Brogan house seemed full of happiness. Robin felt almost lighthearted as he helped the twins design a gravestone for Chop Bone Man. He was beginning to allow himself to feel safe at last. Perry and Ant, who considered themselves in mourning, found his cheerfulness quite oppressive.

"You wouldn't think you were helping to make a gravestone for one of your friends!" complained Ant.

"Sorry," said Robin.

Mrs. Brogan also was happy. She had arranged that

Robin should have a surprise that evening and when the twins came around after lunch and suggested they go into the town for gravestone paint ("'Chop Bone Man' is too long a name to carve," explained Perry. "We'll have to paint it, especially if we're going to put a poem on as well!"), she agreed that it might be sensible to stock up on dog biscuits at the same time, instead of making squashing remarks about waiting and seeing.

"What about Sun Dance?" Robin asked before they set off.

"Mum said to leave him," replied Ant. "She said he's settled with his book and she wants him kept that way. He's to have a quiet day today."

Whatever Dan's faults, and they were many, he was a dedicated and enthusiastic beachcomber. Mrs. Brogan said this proved that he was not all bad. When bed and breakfasting permitted she was a devoted beachcomber herself and she said all beachcombers were hard working, optimistic, and highly intelligent.

It was amazing what one could find. Buckets and spades in great quantity. Wood of all descriptions that made driftwood fires which burned with blue flames and left a fine and fragrant ash all over the house. Half-full cans of grease were washed up and paint lost overboard from ships (which was the reason that so many of the houses in the town were painted battleship gray). Ropes, onions, hearthbrushes, T-shirts, and a thousand other things all appeared from time to time, but best of all, as far as Dan was concerned, one could find money. People were always dropping loose coins from their pockets as they changed in and out of swimsuits, or sat down to eat, or ran about. The money would sink out of sight, hidden beneath a shallow layer of sand until a windy day blew the sand away and the coins would be left exposed. Pocket knives and keyrings sometimes emerged in the same way, but it was the money that Dan liked best, and early and late, according to wind and tide, he searched for it.

The only way down to the beach was through the wide opening in the cliffs opposite the Robinson and Brogan houses. Dan, being an opportunist, never failed to look over the garden walls as he passed to see what was going on. Since he had caught Robin red-handed stealing from the shop, Robin had become much, much easier to aggravate, and when the twins were not about, Sun Dance was even better. It was very, very easy to bait Sun Dance. His hackles rose on every possible occasion.

Sun Dance was sitting reading on the grass in front of the house. He was very lonely. Mrs. Robinson had instructed everyone not to overexcite him and so they had left him alone. Nobody, not even Sun Dance, knew exactly what had caused the latest attack of panic-stricken screaming, but nobody wanted it repeated. He had been kept in bed half the morning while everyone else had a lovely time constructing a gravestone, and now they had gone into town without him. He was very pleased when Dan looked over the garden wall.

"Hello!" he said.

"Now, now!" replied Dan reprovingly. "Remember Mummy! Musn't speak to big bad Dan! That's what she told you!"

"She's always telling me things," said Sun Dance.

"She says I've got to read quietly but I need someone to practice on."

"Practice what?"

Sun Dance showed him his book. It was called *Teach Yourself Self-Defense*. He had borrowed it from Perry who had acquired it in a job lot when he swapped his new sweatshirt for a bike lamp and some old books.

"I can't work it out on my own," he told Dan. "You need someone to practice on."

"Practice on those soppy twins," suggested Dan. "Or that useless Brogan kid!"

"Perry and Ant have gone into town to buy gravestone paint."

"Gravestone paint!" repeated Dan incredulously.

"For Chop Bone Man's grave."

"Chop Bone Man!" said Dan.

"Don't keep copying everything I say! And Robin's gone with them to buy stuff for his dog."

"What?" said Dan.

"Stuff for his dog."

"What dog?" asked Dan, enormously surprised.

"Robin's dog," repeated Sun Dance. "Are you deaf? He's getting him tomorrow!"

"What, old Scared of Dogs is getting a dog! I don't believe it!"

"Well, he is!"

"They're stuffing you with nonsense," said Dan. "I'd believe in gravestone paint before I believed Robin Brogan is getting a dog!"

"You'll see tomorrow when Friday is here," said Sun Dance.

"Robin Brogan is scared of dogs," stated Dan. "He's teasing you! He knows how nutty you are! I bet there's no such dog!"

"Well, you'd be wrong!" said Sun Dance furiously.

"As if anyone could believe anything you said!" scoffed Dan.

"It's perfectly true!"

"Oh yes!"

"Yes! I saw him! We found him on the beach! Wait there! I've just remembered!"

"Remembered what?"

"He's even in the paper! Lost and Found! He's written down, I read it there last night!" And Sun Dance tore inside, grabbed the paper from under his mattress, and returned to shove it delightedly under Dan's scornful nose.

"I knew I'd forgotten something from yesterday!" said Sun Dance, and he danced up and down while Dan read:

LOST AND FOUND
LOST: Black Spaniel Type Dog
Answers to the name of Keeper
Contact: BROWN, 2 Abbey Lane, Eastcliffe.
Telephone: 555-6814
REWARD!

"See! That's proof!" shouted Sun Dance.

"'Reward!'" read Dan out loud.

Sun Dance stopped dancing and felt suddenly cold and sick. Of course! Now he remembered why he had screamed in the night! Someone was looking for Friday.

"Reward?" asked Dan. "Reward?" And he jumped over the garden wall to look more closely.

All at once Sun Dance knew what he had done. Lost Robin his dog on the very last day.

"I bet that's the dead dog I found on the beach!" said Dan.

"It isn't!" stammered Sun Dance, beginning desperately to lie. "He wasn't dead! It's another dog!"

"How d'you know that?" asked Dan.

"Anyway, the police have got that dog," said Sun Dance.

"Let me look again," ordered Dan.

"No!" Sun Dance clutched the paper tightly. "It's the wrong dog!"

"It said 'Reward,'" persisted Dan.

"Not for Robin's dog, though," replied Sun Dance. "Robin never got a reward. Anyway, it's too late now! It's seven days today! Ancient laws will count again!"

Dan made a grab for the paper.

"If Robin Brogan handed that dog I found in to the police and hasn't claimed the reward then I'm going to," he said. "I found it first anyway! Give me that paper!"

Then Sun Dance went completely mad. He hit Dan with the book on self-defense, sank his teeth into Dan's grabbing hand, and, hugging the paper to his chest, kicked Dan swiftly on his shins and started running. He did not think where he would go and he did not wonder what would happen next. He simply ran and Dan followed, out of the garden, across the slope that led down to the beach, and along the cliff path, where he was forbidden to go because it was not safe.

Sun Dance was enjoying himself. Dan was strong and long-legged but Sun Dance was quick and light. He could run so much faster than Dan that he had time to turn around every so often and make rude and jeering remarks. Whenever he did this Dan lurched to grab him, stumbled, and became more and more infuriated. Just to hear him puff and swear filled Sun Dance with delicious joy.

The cliff path was not safe. It was continually collapsing and the council was always fencing off the worst bits and putting up warning notices. Every time the tides were particularly high a bit more of the underneath of the cliffs would be battered by the waves and break away, and then the soil on top would begin to crumble and another chunk of path would slide over the edge. Local people wrote letters to the council saying something must be done and the council printed replies in the newspapers and sometimes put up a few more fences and notices. Really nothing could be done and everyone knew it. There was no way of stopping the wind and the waves and the tide.

Mrs. Brogan always warned her guests about the cliff path, even the guests she did not like very much, and when the Robinsons moved next door she warned them too. Mr. and Mrs. Robinson listened and were careful. One afternoon they even took their children right along it and showed them how dangerous it could be and explained why they must never use it. All the Robinson children had promised faithfully that they never would.

Since then they had dug for bones and strung them up beneath their neighbor's bed-and-breakfast sign, they had painted the dog, dropped eggs in the library, given tomatoes to tramps, slept with homemade skeletons, fallen through the greenhouse roof, and tried to burgle the police station, but they had kept their promise and stayed away from the path along the cliffs.

Sun Dance forgot that there had ever been such a promise. He sprinted along, waving the paper above his head and calling Dan names.

"You little devil!" panted Dan.

"Bloody-nosed burglar," yelled Sun Dance. "Bloody-nosed burglar! You'll get caught by ancient laws!"

"You wait!" Dan made another dive at Sun Dance and once again Sun Dance jumped nimbly out of reach, but this time he was not lucky. Before he could stop himself he had slipped on the long damp grass at the edge of the cliff. He shrieked, scrambled wildly and was gone. In another moment Dan, seeing the danger, but too late to do anything about it, plunged after him.

All Dan's past, misspent life flashed through his mind as he fell. It was interesting and diverted his thoughts from death and he did not regret a moment of it, except, of course, for the very last step on the cliff.

Nothing passed through Sun Dance's mind. It never occurred to him for one moment that he was in any real danger and he was right.

If they had chosen it on purpose they could not have found a better place to fall. The storms of the previous winter had broken a half-moon-shaped piece of the path away, and it had slipped, but not fallen. It hung six or seven feet down from the edge of the cliff, held in place by nothing much, but all in one piece and with grass still growing on it. Sun Dance landed on all fours on this patch of grass but Dan slid down the crack between Sun Dance's perch and the cliff. He jammed just above his knees.

"Got you now!" said Sun Dance and regarded Dan with pleasure.

"Bloody mess!" said Dan.

"Yes," agreed Sun Dance.

"Are you all right?" asked Dan, proving that Mrs. Brogan had been quite right when she had said that he was not all bad.

"I'm fine," Sun Dance answered cheerfully. "You're not, though, are you?"

"I'm stuck," said Dan.

"Yes, I know," replied Sun Dance and he bounced with satisfaction upon his bit of grass. As he bounced there was an ominous creaking sound followed by the patter of crumbs of earth landing on the rocky beach far below them. Dan found that his legs were suddenly much looser.

"Don't move!" he said in anguish. "You'll bring the whole lot down if you do! Come away from the edge!"

Sun Dance deliberately bounced again to see if Dan was telling the truth. Once again the ground moved unnervingly. Thoroughly frightened, he scuttled away from the edge and clutched Dan's arm.

"Keep still and let me think!" said Dan.

"Will it move again?"

"I don't think so if you keep dead still. It's when you rock at the outside edge it loosens."

"Do you think anyone will come and rescue us?"

"No one knows that we need rescuing, do they?"

"Perhaps someone will come along the path."

"Hardly anyone comes along here," said Dan. "It's not safe. People go round by the beach."

"What if we're still here and it gets dark?"

Dan did not answer. It was not darkness that worried him. Darkness would be very unpleasant, but no more awful than that. High tide would be infinitely worse. Then the waves would be breaking underneath them, and for all he knew would bring their bit of cliff top down altogether. It had been loosened far too much already that afternoon.

"Listen!" he said eventually. "We can't stay here!"

"No," agreed Sun Dance dolefully.

"And I'm stuck fast. I've got my feet in a sort of ledge but I can't move my legs properly. I daren't try, anyway, in case it all comes down. I can't get out but you could!"

"Could I?" asked Sun Dance, cheering up at once. "How?"

"Stand up and see how far you can reach," said Dan.

Sun Dance, by stretching, found that he could just touch the top of the cliff with his fingertips.

"If you got onto my shoulders, could you get your elbows on the edge and heave yourself up like climbing over a wall?"

"No!" said Sun Dance firmly. "You might collapse!"

"I won't. I'm all right if I don't move sideways. It

would only take a minute and then you'd be up on the path and could go and fetch help."

"What will happen if we just stay here?"

"I don't know. I know what I think might happen, though."

"What?"

"The tide will come in and break down this bit we're stuck on from underneath and we'll both go straight over onto the rocks."

"Oh," said Sun Dance.

"So are you going to climb up?"

"It might not happen."

Dan admitted that but said he didn't fancy waiting to see if Sun Dance was right and added that it would be dark at high tide and the sea got quite deep on that part of the coast. Put like that it seemed to Sun Dance that he had very little choice. With Dan's help he clambered gingerly onto his shoulders, reached up, and in a moment was rolling safely on the grassy path. Nothing Sun Dance had ever known felt so good as the solid earth beneath his body.

"Now," called Dan from beneath, "go and fetch someone! Try and find Robin's mum if you can, she knows all about these cliffs! But don't run!"

"No," said Sun Dance.

"Walk. Go carefully but be as quick as you can! Don't for goodness sake fall over the edge again."

"I won't," said Sun Dance.

There followed what seemed to Dan to be hours and hours of silence. He rubbed his aching shoulders. Sun Dance had kicked them very hard when he climbed up—

not entirely by accident, Dan suspected. He hoped very much that the Robinson kid would get home safely. It was a horrible place to have to wait. Dan made the mistake of looking down and immediately wished he hadn't. He closed his eyes after that and began to use his ears instead, listening hopefully for the sound of footsteps or perhaps voices calling, but there was nothing to be heard except the waves below and the occasional cry of a sea gull. He wondered how long it would take for Sun Dance to find someone who could help. It seemed as if he had been wedged in his crack for weeks.

Suddenly he heard a different noise. A sort of scuffle in the grass above him. The sort of sound a rabbit might make, but Dan had a horrible feeling that it was not a rabbit. It was followed by a bored, tuneless humming. Rabbits did not hum, thought Dan, and was suddenly frightened.

"Hello!" he called.

"Hello!" said Sun Dance, peering over the edge.

Dan stared at him in disbelief.

"Why are you still here?" he demanded furiously.

"I just am," replied Sun Dance.

"I thought you'd gone ages ago!"

"I thought you had," replied Sun Dance. "I was just getting up to check!"

"Where did you think I'd gone?"

"You were so quiet I thought you must have fallen over the edge," explained Sun Dance calmly. "I was worried in case you had and you'd landed on the sand and walked back and telephoned that number in the paper and got Robin's dog's reward! But you're still stuck, aren't you?"

"I can't believe I'm hearing this!" said Dan.

"Why not?" asked Sun Dance.

"You must be crazy!"

"I'm not!" said Sun Dance indignantly. "I've thought out what to do! Everything will be all right because if you stay here you won't be able to tell anyone about Robin's dog and if I stay here I won't tell anyone you've fallen off the cliff like I might do by mistake if I went home. So that's what we're going to do!"

"WHAT!" yelled Dan.

"It's only till morning!" said Sun Dance.

seven

● ● ● ● ● ● ●

Every quarter of an hour or so Mrs. Robinson had been glancing out of the front door to see if Sun Dance was still where he was meant to be, sitting on the doorstep reading his book.

"I thought it was too good to be true!" she exclaimed when she discovered his disappearance. She noticed the garden gate was wide open and hurried to look up and down the road, but Sun Dance was nowhere in sight. Back in the house she called his name. There was no reply.

Mrs. Robinson began to feel slightly uneasy. The house was very quiet but when she stepped out into the garden she could hear Beany's high, excited voice calling Mrs. Brogan's name from over the garden wall.

"More bed and breakfasters on the phone!" Beany was announcing excitedly. "They say they've got four ordinary children and can they stay for a week. They want to talk to you!"

Mrs. Brogan hurried indoors. It was the third book-ing that morning, and the second from people proudly claiming to have ordinary children.

"They sound nice!" Beany told her as she handed over the receiver.

They did sound nice. They were a family with rela-tives in the town and wanted somewhere to stay while they visited them. Someone had given them Mrs. Bro-gan's telephone number. Mrs. Brogan made a note of the booking and put down the receiver feeling slightly puz-zled.

"Who did they ask for?" she asked Beany.

"My mum," said Beany, "but I told them I didn't live here so then they said was this Porridge Hall and could they speak to the owner so I went and got you."

"Everyone this morning has asked for Porridge Hall," said Mrs. Brogan. "I can't think why. I wonder where they've got the old name from."

"It's up on the wall," said Beany. "And it's a much nicer name than Sea View! Dad says you should never have changed it!"

"Perhaps I ought to change back," said Mrs. Brogan. "Hello! Here's your mother!"

"There you are! I thought I heard voices," exclaimed Mrs. Robinson, spotting Beany with relief. "Where's Sun Dance hiding? I told him to stay put."

"Not here," Mrs. Brogan told her. "Is something wrong?"

"I don't suppose so," replied Mrs. Robinson, "but I've misplaced Sun Dance. I thought he might be here . . . I guessed you had Beany . . . are you sure you're not being a nuisance, Beany? . . . You must come back home if Mrs. Brogan's busy . . . I left him sitting in the front garden, good as gold. Have you seen him?"

"I don't think I've noticed him all day," said Mrs. Brogan. "I've been tidying up the garden and Beany's been manning the phone for me. Could he have gone after the twins and Robin?"

"He's in trouble if he has," said Mrs. Robinson grimly, and she went back home to search the house again. Mrs. Brogan and Beany crossed the road to see if they could see him on the beach, and then Mrs. Brogan had an awful thought that he might be entangled in the remains of the greenhouse next door and rushed round to check. She found that her neighbor had had the same idea.

"Thank goodness for that, anyway!" she exclaimed.

"I'm sure I'm worrying about nothing," said Mrs. Robinson.

"Perhaps Old Blanket could track him down," suggested Beany hopefully, and she woke Old Blanket, who was snoring on Perry's quilt, and gave him Sun Dance's pajamas to sniff. Old Blanket inspected them carefully and led the way to the cookie jar.

"He thinks he's in there," said Beany.

"He doesn't," said her mother crossly. "He's just greedy! Has he been sleeping on the beds again?"

"Only Perry's," said Beany, giving Old Blanket a cookie.

"Don't give him chocolate ones! He's too fat already!"

Old Blanket and Beany looked reproachfully at her but she took no notice. By the time the twins and Robin arrived back home she had worked herself up into what Mrs. Brogan described as "a state." "Isn't Sun Dance with you?" she demanded, rushing out to meet them.

"'Course not," said Perry. "You said to leave him alone."

"We thought he might have followed after you," said his mother.

They shook their heads and looked blank.

"What do you want him for?" asked Ant.

"He's lost," explained Beany. "Old Blanket tracked him as far as the cookie jar but then he got stuck."

"Sun Dance doesn't eat cookies," said Ant. "He eats tomatoes. Have you looked in the fridge?"

"Don't be silly, Ant!" said Mrs. Robinson. "Could you have passed him in town?"

"Easily," Perry told her. "It was really crowded. Do you want us to go back and look for him?" He suddenly remembered Sun Dance's visit to the police station and wondered if his reckless little brother had been tempted to try his luck again.

"It's not as if there's that many shops to lose him in," said Mrs. Robinson worriedly. "You might check out that little pet shop, though; and Robin, could you have another good look on the beach?"

Robin hurried away at once but he returned quite quickly to say that Sun Dance was nowhere to be seen.

"He'd never wander off along the cliffs, would he?" asked Mrs. Brogan.

"Perhaps he's digging up Chop Bone Man," suggested Beany. "He said he was going to!"

"The little monkey!" exclaimed Mrs. Robinson. "But

we've looked in the garden already. I'm sure we'd have noticed him." Nevertheless she went off to check.

"I'm sure I'm making a fuss about nothing," she admitted. "He'd never go near the cliffs. He knows better. I expect the twins will be back with him any minute."

"I'll go and look on the beach again," said Robin.

For a long time he gazed backwards and forwards along the sand. There was still no sign of Sun Dance at all, and Robin was turning to go home when a distant flash of light caught his eye, far along the coast, on one of the jutting headlands. It was so uncannily familiar that Robin stood waiting to see if it would happen again. He knew it was something that he had seen before, not once, but often. Very often. As he stared at the spot where it had appeared it suddenly glinted again. It was somewhere along the cliff path.

The cliff path was as forbidden to Robin as it was to the Robinson children, but in spite of that he started to follow its winding length. He was nearly halfway along before he realized that what he had seen was the sunlight reflecting off Sun Dance's spectacles. All at once he began to hurry.

As he drew closer he could see Sun Dance himself. He was leaning in a perilous position over the edge of the cliff and he was talking to someone. Odd words came floating along the breeze to Robin. Sun Dance was lecturing whoever it was on his favorite subject.

"Ancient laws!" Robin heard. "They'll count again! Seven days will be gone tomorrow. You've only got to stay there till then."

There was a reply that Robin did not catch but it

seemed to offend Sun Dance because, much to Robin's relief, he shuffled back from the edge of the cliff, leaned himself against a nearby fencepost, and appeared to go to sleep.

"Sun Dance!" shouted Robin.

Sun Dance opened his eyes and looked up.

"What are you doing?" demanded Robin. "Your mum's going nuts looking for you!"

"I've got a surprise," said Sun Dance proudly. "Look over the edge and you'll see it!"

But Robin, who had heard a call that seemed to come from the ground beneath his feet, was already lying down to look over the cliff. He found himself staring into Dan's eyes.

"Good grief!" said Robin.

Dan did not waste time on explanations or greetings. "Listen!" he said. "High tide will be up in half an hour. Then the sea will be breaking right underneath me and I'm sure this bit of ground is getting looser. My legs were stuck tight but I can move them quite easily now."

"Don't listen to him!" said Sun Dance earnestly. "He's just saying it so we'll get him up. It's quite safe down there if you don't bounce about! I fell over too, but I got up again all right!"

"He's mad! I'm sure he is! He's been sitting up there talking rubbish for hours!" said Dan.

"How did you manage to get up?" Robin asked Sun Dance.

"I climbed on Dan's shoulders," said Sun Dance shamelessly. "Wasn't I brave?"

Robin looked down and Dan looked up and for the first time in their lives they regarded each other with complete understanding. Sun Dance seemed to have no idea at all of the disgracefulness of his behavior, but it did not seem a good moment to try and explain it to him.

"Have you got a belt or something?" asked Dan. "I can manage to get loose but I daren't try and move very much without something to hold on to."

"I've got much better than a belt," Robin told him, and to Sun Dance's dismay he produced from his pocket the extra long, extra strong dog leash that he had bought for Friday. The man who had sold it to Robin had been right when he said it would hold almost anything. With one end around the fencepost and the other around Dan's wrists, it held while Robin pulled and Dan scrambled and Sun Dance, reluctantly obeying Robin's orders, tugged casually with one hand and argued that it was all unnecessary.

"I don't see why we can't leave him there a bit longer," he grumbled. It was not until Dan gave one last kick and the whole broken-off bit of grass and cliff suddenly tumbled into the sea that he changed his mind. Yelping with fright he pulled so hard that Dan shot over the cliff top and landed on his nose.

For a long time, exactly as Sun Dance had done, Dan sprawled on the grass and hugged the solid ground. When he came to himself he found that someone was patting his back and congratulating him on his recovery.

"Don't worry!" Sun Dance was saying kindly. "I got you up! You'll be all right now!"

Dan rolled over and goggled at him in disbelief.

"Your nose is bleeding," said Sun Dance, worriedly inspecting Dan's face.

"I banged it getting over the edge," said Dan. "It bleeds easily!"

Robin grinned self-consciously at this remark, and then suddenly remembered the search that was going on at home.

"Your mum's been looking for you for ages!" he told Sun Dance. "Come on! We'd better get back before she calls the police!"

"Is she cross?" asked Sun Dance.

"Very," said Robin. "And she'll be worse when she finds out where you were!"

"She won't mind when she hears what I've been doing," said Sun Dance cheerfully.

"She'll go howling mad when she hears what you've been doing," said Robin, but Sun Dance said he thought not.

"Not when she hears how I rescued Dan," he explained.

"You what?" asked Dan.

"Rescued you," said Sun Dance. "Didn't I?" But he did not wait for a reply. Abandoning Robin and Dan he hopped happily away, dashing a little distance along the path and then pausing to wait, completely disregarding Robin and Dan's commands to walk carefully.

"You'll be over the edge again!" said Dan, stopping in the middle of his account of the afternoon to watch Sun Dance as he balanced on one foot like a tightrope walker.

"We ought to put him on that leash!" said Dan.

"Come back and walk with us before you fall off!" shouted Robin.

"I'm not falling off!" said Sun Dance, and Robin,

watching closely, could see that this was true. Sun Dance's steps might look as random as raindrops falling in a puddle, but they were being as carefully calculated as the bed-and-breakfast accounts. Robin could see that he was perfectly safe, engrossed as wholeheartedly in not falling off the cliff as he ever had been in the troubles of tramps or the validity of ancient laws. Dan did not realize this. He looked at Sun Dance, dancing with death along the cliff edge and said,

"I'm surprised they ever let him out!"

"I don't suppose they ever will again," said Robin. "Not when his mum hears about this afternoon."

"What do you think she'll do? Mine would give me a good belting!"

"She won't do that! She'll just never let him out of her sight again!"

"Oh," said Dan, to whom freedom meant more than comfort or safety. "Poor old kid, then! I'd rather have the belting!" And he plodded on in silence for a while.

"Sorry about your nose," said Robin, somewhere toward the end of the path.

"Told you, I bashed it getting over."

"I meant the other times. I didn't know it bled really easily."

"S'pose you thought it was your fantastic punching!"

"Yes, I did," said Robin, disappointed but truthful.

"Huh!" said Dan, but then, moved perhaps by Robin's honesty, added, "I wouldn't have said anything about that dog if I'd known you were that bothered. I just thought I might as well get the reward. I couldn't make out half that kid was talking about."

"Not many people can, I don't think," said Robin, and went on to tell Dan about Friday and the seven awful days of waiting, and even about the notice in the shop window, and the Moores who had come bed and breakfasting and told him about the dog they had lost. It was a relief to tell someone, especially Dan, who did not constantly interrupt with impractical plans, as the twins would have done, or try to comfort him, as his mother would have.

Dan listened in silence until Robin reached the second unanswered telephone call and then merely remarked, "You're too soft! I would never have phoned them!"

"What else could I do?"

"Say nothing," said Dan. "They'd never have known."

"The police could have told them."

"Well, you shouldn't have given him to the police in the first place."

"I didn't, Mum did."

"Shouldn't have let her," said Dan firmly, but when Robin asked how he could possibly have stopped her Dan was silent. He had not yet found a way of stopping his own mother doing the things she felt she ought.

"Look!" said Dan suddenly.

Sun Dance had reached the end of the cliff path at last and out of nowhere a crowd of his relatives appeared. They seized Sun Dance and Robin and Dan and held them and demanded explanations.

"You promised me, *you promised me*, that you would

never go along that path!" scolded Mrs. Robinson, clutching Sun Dance by the shoulders and hugging and shaking him at the same time.

"Dan's nose bled like mad!" said Sun Dance, wriggling out of reach.

"You've been fighting!"

"We haven't!" said Sun Dance and Robin and Dan, indignantly and all together, and they did not even consider that chasing people off cliffs and planning to leave them there all night might be thought of as fighting.

"What exactly has been going on, Robin?" asked Mrs. Robinson.

"Well . . ." said Robin, and stopped.

"Yes?"

"I'm not exactly sure how it began," said Robin, "but . . ."

"Dan fell off the cliff!" interrupted Sun Dance. "And guess who stayed at the top and pulled him up with Robin's dog leash! Yes! And the bit of cliff that Dan was on all smashed down into the sea!"

"You might have been killed!" exclaimed Mrs. Robinson, and she looked as angry with Dan as she had with Sun Dance a moment before.

"And I pulled him up!" continued Sun Dance. "And he shot over the top back onto the path and bashed his nose. Good job I was there!"

"Robin, is this true?" demanded Mrs. Robinson.

"Well, I pulled too," said Robin. "But Sun Dance did help!"

"If I hadn't been there you wouldn't even have known where Dan was!" protested Sun Dance.

"S'pose not," agreed Robin, and Dan, most unaccountably, said nothing at all, even when the twins and Beany crowded round the immodest Sun Dance and hailed him as a hero.

"Let's get away while they're still all talking," muttered Dan to Robin, and Robin nodded in agreement and hurried Dan under the bed-and-breakfast sign and into the Brogans' front garden before Mrs. Robinson could ask any more questions.

"D'you think he might get away with it?" asked Dan, looking back at Sun Dance.

"Hope so," said Robin. "'Specially as he was trying to save Friday for me. And nobody's hurt, except your nose."

"That's nothing," said Dan. "But do you know what? He really thinks he pulled me up! He really does!"

"'Course he does," agreed Robin tolerantly. "He'll probably be your friend for life now, whether you like it or not! You'd better come in and wash some of that blood off before your mum sees you."

He pushed open the front door and was struck by the quietness. No radio, or television, or sound of clattering in the kitchen, or voices, or footsteps. It was as if the house was waiting for him.

"That you, Robin?" called his mother from the kitchen. "Beany told me Sun Dance was in sight so I came back in. Is everyone all right?"

"Yes," shouted Robin. "I've just brought Dan back to . . ."

"Shut the front door!" called his mother, and a moment later there was a crash and a pattering of feet across the tiles and a small black dog shot across the hall and into Robin's arms.

"I knew he'd remember you," said Mrs. Brogan with satisfaction. "He remembered me the moment he saw me! Hello, Dan! Have you been in the wars?"

"'Sonly my nose," said Dan self-consciously. "Robin said I could come in and wash it. I thought the seven days weren't up until tomorrow."

"I telephoned this morning and they said we could have him tonight," explained Mrs. Brogan. "I nipped out and collected him this afternoon. I wouldn't have gone, but I half expected to find Sun Dance there before me! Are you sure he's all right?"

"He's fine," said Robin, down on his knees and trying to fend off Friday's slobbering tongue. "He's busy being a hero for rescuing Dan! Isn't he, Dan?"

"Oh yes," agreed Dan, glancing from Robin to Mrs. Brogan uncertainly. "He's out there telling them all about it."

"What was he rescuing you from, Dan?" asked Robin's mother.

Dan, after trying but failing to think of an unalarming reply to this question, treated Mrs. Brogan to the glassy-eyed stare he usually reserved for his teachers.

"Don't say you've forgotten?" said Mrs. Brogan.

Dan was just about to admit that this was indeed the case when Robin interrupted.

"He slipped, didn't you, Dan? And Sun Dance pulled him up."

"Is that all?" asked Mrs. Brogan disappointedly.

"More or less," said Dan.

"Well, wash off the blood and ring your mother and ask if you can stay to supper," said Mrs. Brogan. "I can see that I've been told all that I'm going to get! And Robin hasn't said a word yet about my wonderful surprise!"

"His leg's better," said Robin.

"He still needs feeding up," said Mrs. Brogan. "Give me your sweater, Dan, and I'll put it to soak before the blood dries completely. You can squeeze into one of Robin's to go home. Are you *sure* Sun Dance was the hero of this affair?"

"Mum!" said Robin, while Dan pulled the sweater over his head and stayed inside it until the question was over.

"All right, all right!" said Mrs. Brogan, and Dan hurried upstairs to the bathroom before she could say anything more.

"Thanks very much for getting Friday," said Robin. "Very much! He looks loads better."

"What's bothering you then, Robin?" asked Mrs. Brogan. "I thought you'd be over the moon."

"I am!" said Robin.

"You're not!" said his mother.

"Well, it's just that I can't help thinking about the people who owned him. What if they still want him back?"

"They've had all week to look and ask and advertise," his mother said firmly. "I'm sure he was abandoned, poor little dog. The twins thought so right at the beginning, didn't they, and the vet who saw to his leg thought the same."

"Did he?"

"Yes, so cheer up! Look at his coat! It's going to be quite long, I think. What sort do you think he is?"

"The twins thought he was a sort of spaniel," said Robin.

"That's what the vet said," agreed Mrs. Brogan. "A bit of something else, but spaniel type."

Robin jumped as if something had suddenly hurt him but luckily at that moment Dan appeared at the top of the stairs holding his nose protectively.

"I'm very sorry but it's started again," he said, and in the intervening few minutes of blood and apologies Robin had time to pull himself together.

They had a cheerful supper, and afterward Mrs. Brogan suggested they should take Friday next door for a few minutes, but neither Robin nor Dan looked at all enthusiastic.

"Do you mind if we don't?" asked Robin. "Just for tonight? Mrs. Robinson will only start asking questions again . . ."

"Ah," said Mrs. Brogan. "The heroic Sun Dance! Perhaps you're right!"

Dan looked relieved, and Robin even more so. He could not imagine the effect on Sun Dance of seeing Friday again if Friday was going to have to disappear once more. Robin was trying to force himself to do something very difficult and the fewer people who were affected the better.

The evening grew later and it was time for Dan to go home. They stood in the darkening garden with Friday between them and Dan said, "Well, you got your dog."

"Yes," agreed Robin, but he stroked Friday's back uncertainly as he spoke.

"All you've got to do," said Dan, reading his thoughts, "is to keep him away from that address in the paper. And perhaps don't take him into town in case you meet them."

"Yes," said Robin, "and perhaps not down to the beach in case I see them there, or anywhere else, either. And I'll be wondering all the time who they are and if he's still safe."

"S'pose there's nothing else you can do," said Dan, and he bent and rubbed Friday's head.

"It's not going to be much fun," said Robin.

"No," agreed Dan thoughtfully.

Robin suddenly made up his mind.

"I'm going to see them," he announced. "I'll tell them I've got Friday and I'll tell them what I think of the way they've treated him and I'll offer to buy him. That was what Mum said she'd do if anyone claimed him. And I'm going now! I can't wait another night!"

"I'll come with you," said Dan. "And if I were you I wouldn't take Friday. Make them come and collect him if they want him that much."

Robin thought that was a good idea and took Friday back into the house.

"Where's that paper with the address?" he asked Dan when he came back out again.

"Sun Dance had it," said Dan, "at least he had it when he fell. I bet he dropped it! It's probably floating out to sea by now. Doesn't your mum get one?"

"No," said Robin.

"We'd better go and get ours then," said Dan.

That was not as easy as it sounded. It was long past the time Dan should have been home already, and his mother was most reluctant to let him back out again. Robin, waiting in the street outside the house, had almost given up hope when Dan finally reappeared.

"You should have come in," said Dan. "Why didn't you?"

"I didn't want to have to start explaining again. And besides, what about your nose?"

"What about it?"

"Your mum didn't like me bashing it much," replied Robin diffidently.

Dan grinned suddenly. "She'd have stopped me coming if she could," he told Robin. "But Dad's home and when I said where I was going he let me."

Dan stopped suddenly and went dusky red under his sunburn, realizing that he had used the taboo word again, but Robin did not seem to have noticed.

"Sorry!" said Dan.

"What for?"

"Talking about my dad."

"Why shouldn't you?" asked Robin, surprised.

Dan went even redder.

"Because yours . . . because he . . . your dad was . . ."

"Was killed," said Robin calmly. "It's all right to say it! Why did your dad decide you could come?"

"It was when I told him who I was going with," explained Dan. "He knew your dad. They were friends or something, when they were at school. Before Dad started truck driving."

"I didn't know your dad was a truck driver."

"That's why he's never home," said Dan.

"Did your dad know when mine was killed?" asked Robin curiously.

"'Course he did! I remember the day! It was awful! It was the day we were supposed to go on holiday and we didn't go."

"Why not?"

"Because Dad was too fed up. We'd been going to Scotland. We were going to get a boat but we never went." Even now, two years later, Dan could still feel the miserable disappointment of that abandoned holiday. Robin could hear it in his voice.

"You should have gone," he said.

"Doesn't matter now," replied Dan, and realized that at last it really didn't. "Dad said to bring you round one day," he added, and was surprised to see how pleased Robin looked.

All the time they had been talking, Dan had noticed that Robin was walking faster and faster, so that when they finally reached the turning for Abbey Lane he was almost running.

"Hey! Slow down a bit!" he said breathlessly.

"Sorry!" said Robin.

They turned a corner and the house stood before them. In front of the lighted windows of number two they paused to gather their courage.

"What'll I do if they won't sell him?" asked Robin.

Dan held his head in his hands and thought and thought.

"I'll ask my dad," he said eventually, and Robin

did not appear to think this too bad an idea.

"Come on then," he said, but before they could do anything further the front door of the house opened and a light shone into the garden. Into the light waddled a fat black heap, and after it came a thin old lady.

"Not too far, Keeper!" she called. "We don't want to lose you again!"

She caught sight of Robin and Dan, staring at the black heap with their mouths open.

"Hello!" she said.

Dan found his voice first.

"Is that your dog?" he demanded.

"Yes," she replied, "that's Keeper!"

"The one that you put up the notice about and the ad in the newspaper for?" asked Robin.

"That's right," she agreed. "Well, we put up dozens of notices, actually, not just one. Yes, he came wandering home three days ago but we didn't get around to canceling the ad, I'm afraid."

Robin and Dan continued to stare as she collected the huge hairy heap and herded it back into the house. It was certainly black, and it answered (with groans) to the name of Keeper and it might even once have resembled a spaniel (before it ate so much), but it was nothing like Friday, or any other dog that either Robin or Dan had ever seen.

"To think I nearly died for that!" said Dan indignantly.

"Yes!" said Robin, and he danced as wildly under the streetlamps as Sun Dance had done on the cliff.

"It looked like a heap of old coats!" said Dan in disgust. "Anyway, you can stop worrying now! You've got your dog! Stop jumping about so much! That old woman is watching you through the window!"

Robin stopped his wild leaping and returned to his usual quiet self, except that inside he was shouting with happiness.

"You wouldn't think you'd ever been scared of dogs," said Dan, ambling along beside him. "What are you grinning about?"

"I was just thinking how pleased Sun Dance will be."

"Sun Dance!" repeated Dan. "Hey! I know what I meant to ask you! Something he kept talking about! Someone they've buried! Chop Bone Man! What did he mean?"

"Come round tomorrow and we'll show you!" said Robin.

eight
●●●●●●●

When summer was nearly over and the autumn storms were beginning to blow, Mrs. Brogan received a letter from Mr. and Mrs. Moore. She read it once, and then she took it around to her next-door neighbors' and read it again.

Dear Mrs. Brogan,
Would it be possible to book a week's visit to you at the end of October? There would be four of us this time; some friends of ours also feel the need of some fresh sea air.

We bought a copy of the local paper as we left East-cliffe in August—we were most impressed by your advertisement! My husband was sure that it could only be the work of your enterprising next-door neighbors! We look forward to meeting the ghosts!

It feels as if we left in the middle of a story. Do give our love to Sun Dance and Beany and Co. We hope so much that Dog Friday came safely back to Robin.

Looking forward to hearing from you!
Very best wishes,
Ann Moore.

P.S. John says to reassure Beany that our friends have plenty of towels of their own and their hair is quite firmly attached to their heads!

"Are those people my bed and breakfasters, then?" asked Beany, very pleased.

"I remember them," said Sun Dance. "The man ate my pudding and cried."

"Everyone's seen that ad," remarked Robin. "People've been seeing ghosts in Porridge Hall all summer! They never did before! What does she mean about our enterprising next-door neighbors?"

"What indeed?" asked Mrs. Brogan. "And I've been blaming you all summer, Robin! Good for Mr. Moore! How could I have been so thick! Perry and Ant! To what do I owe the honor?"

"It was to make up for Chop Bone Man," said Ant, while Perry added, "Well, it worked all right, didn't it?"

"Yes," said Mrs. Brogan. "I shall probably never live it down but it worked all right . . ."

"In the end," said Sun Dance.

"In the end," said Mrs. Brogan.

Hilary McKay is a young English writer. She took a degree in botany and zoology at St. Andrews University and since then has had a variety of jobs, among them farmwork, painting pictures on commission, school librarian, and laboratory work as an analyst. Her first book, *The Exiles*, was hailed by *Kirkus Reviews* as "a delightful debut." It was a 1993 Notable Children's Book in the Language Arts (NCTE); a 1992 Bulletin Blue Ribbon winner (Bulletin of the Center for Children's Books); on the 1992 *Horn Book* Fanfare List; and co-winner of the 1992 *Guardian* Children's Fiction Award in England. Her second book, *The Exiles at Home*, won the 1994 Smarties Prize (U.K.) and, in its paperback edition, was shortlisted for the W. H. Smith Award (U.K.), one of five books. At present Ms. McKay lives and works in Derbyshire, England.

● ● ● ● ●